Naina vibrated with anger and hurt. "I would never do that. Ever. Revealing to anyone what might happen between you and me tonight would be a total betrayal of myself."

Those long fingers of his slid against hers until they were entwined. His touch sent a jolt of warmth up her arm. "I believe you. You've no idea how fantastic that is."

"How?"

He sighed. "I am Vikram Raawal. From the moment I could understand the world, it meant something. It meant more to other people even before I understood what it meant to me. Privilege and power and pride, yes. But so much more that the world doesn't see. Everybody wants something from me. My family, my friends, my fans...apparently even my critics. There are so many expectations that they feel like shackles around my ankles."

He pressed a finger against her mouth when she opened it. "But it's not every day that someone comes to me with no expectations of me. Except maybe what my mouth can do for her."

Naina let her gaze fall to study it. "It *is* a gorgeous mouth," she whispered.

Born into Bollywood

Legends in the limelight meet their match!

Vikram and Virat Rawaal are the uncrowned kings of Bollywood. Born into an influential family that has ruled the Bollywood industry for generations, the time has come for the spotlight to fall firmly on their legacy!

As the world around them glitters, the golden boys of Bollywood hide a family of scandal and deceit. But they are about to discover that once in a lifetime there is someone who can turn their world upside down and cut through the superstardom to the men behind the masks!

A masked ball and a one-night stand are about to set Vikram's world on fire in *Claiming His Bollywood Cinderella*.

And look out for Virat's story
Coming soon!

Tara Pammi

CLAIMING HIS
BOLLYWOOD
CINDERELLA

HARLEQUIN

PRESENTS

HARLEQUIN®
PRESENTS®

Recycling programs
for this product may
not exist in your area.

ISBN-13: 978-1-335-14900-8

Claiming His Bollywood Cinderella

Copyright © 2020 by Tara Pammi

This edition published by arrangement with Harlequin Books S.A.

For questions and comments about the quality of this book,
please contact us at CustomerService@Harlequin.com.

Harlequin Enterprises ULC
22 Adelaide St. West, 40th Floor
Toronto, Ontario M5H 4E3, Canada
www.Harlequin.com

Printed in U.S.A.

Tara Pammi can't remember a moment when she wasn't lost in a book—especially a romance, which was much more exciting than a mathematics textbook at school. Years later, Tara's wild imagination and love for the written word revealed what she really wanted to do. Now she pairs alpha males who think they know everything with strong women who knock that theory and them off their feet!

Books by Tara Pammi

Harlequin Presents

Conveniently Wed!

Sicilian's Bride for a Price

Once Upon a Temptation

The Flaw in His Marriage Plan

Bound to the Desert King

Sheikh's Baby of Revenge

The Scandalous Brunetti Brothers

An Innocent to Tame the Italian
A Deal to Carry the Italian's Heir

Visit the Author Profile page
at Harlequin.com for more titles.

For Megan—for your endless patience and for helping me make this story sparkle while the world was in chaos.

CHAPTER ONE

VIKRAM RAAWAL WALKED up the steps of Raawal Mahal, his family's two-hundred-year-old palatial ancestral bungalow. It was the only property his parents had left unsullied by their still-tempestuous marriage of forty years.

The muggy October afternoon was redolent with the pungent aroma of the jasmine creeper that his grandfather had planted for his wife all those years ago.

His grandparents had shared a love story that couldn't be recreated by all the glittering sets and stars of Bollywood. If not for the fact that Vikram had very clear memories of them—Daadu and Daadi sitting side by side listening to ghazals on the gramophone, sharing stories with him and his younger brother and sister, Daadi keeping silent vigil by her husband's side as he vanished away into nothing…he would have scoffed at even the idea of such a love.

But he had seen it. He'd been a part of it. He'd found comfort and joy in its shadow. And today, at the age of thirty-six, memories of that love hit him hard.

He was lonely, he admitted to himself, as he walked through the gated courtyard toward the main bungalow. The strains of an old ghazal played on the gramophone player, sinking sweetly into his veins, slowly releasing the pent-up tension he'd been carrying. He laughed at the mural his younger brother, Virat, had painted on one wall where a profusion of plants and flowerpots sat on an elevated concrete bench.

The cozy bungalow, full of sweet memories and peaceful childhood associations, was his favorite place in the world. And yet, he had avoided visiting for almost two months, using out-of-country shoots and overloaded scheduling as excuses.

But here in this place where he was just Vikram and not Vikram Raawal, Bollywood star, and the chairman of the family production company Raawal House of Cinema, he couldn't lie to himself.

He hadn't wanted to expose himself to his *daadi*'s brand of perceptiveness. He hadn't wanted her to see how unhappy he'd been of late. How...*unsettled* in his own skin.

The raucous burst of a man's laughter punctured his thoughts. It was Virat.

For a few seconds, Vikram considered turning around and walking out. His recent argument with his brother had been far dirtier than their usual head-butting over projects for Raawal House. Being called arrogant and dominating by a brother that he loved and respected had...shaken him.

The laughter came again and Vikram's curiosity trumped his reluctance. He walked through the grand salon, filled with his grandfather's trophies and accolades from a career that had lasted close to five decades in Bollywood.

Vijay Raawal had not only been a celebrated actor and director but had built his career from the ground up after traveling the country with a theater group for years. Started his own production company, and taken the industry in a new direction. Made mainstream films, art projects, and careers of many stars and never once lost his integrity.

How had his grandfather sustained such a glittering career in such a superficial and cutthroat industry? Had it been simply the unconditional support Daadi had offered him through everything?

After fifteen years and numerous box office hits in Bollywood, Vikram had suddenly found himself filled with a strange feeling of discontent all of a sudden. But it was more than creative burnout. In a cinematic twist, he'd found himself wanting the same kind of support and affection from someone that Daadi had given Daadu while knowing that he wasn't actually capable of returning it.

In a crazy moment of impulse, he'd asked his best friend Zara to marry him. Thankfully, Zara had instantly said no. That he had even considered marriage in the first place—even if it was to his oldest and longest friend, showed how unlike himself he was currently feeling.

He nodded at Ramu Kaka—his grandfather's old manservant, as old and comfortably familiar as the bungalow itself.

The first thing that hit him as he entered the expansive sitting room was the subtle scent of roses. Every inch of him stilled as he stood over the threshold, his long form hidden from his *daadi* and Virat by the L-shaped angle of the hall. They were lounging on the divan, while a number of their servants stood huddled by the other door that led to the huge kitchen. Every mouth twitched in varying degrees of smiles.

In the middle of the room, kneeling on the rug, was a young woman with her face in profile to Vikram. Evening sunlight filtered through the high windows in the room and lit up her silhouette. The first thing he noted was the dark halo of her hair, curly and thick like her very own crown, that swung from side to side every time she moved her head, and huge glittering earrings that reminded him of the crystal chandelier Mama had spent thousands of dollars on in some Italian boutique.

The earrings swayed enchantingly every time the young woman moved her head. And she did it a lot. His mouth curved.

Wide eyes, pert nose and a lush mouth moved in constant animation, along with her plump body. Almost anesthetized by seeing size zero bodies on movie sets, he let his gaze return to the voluptuous lines of her body with a curious fascination. A white cotton kurta hugged her breasts, a long chain of glittery beads dancing over them.

White stones on tiny half-moon gold hoops glinted in a perfect line over the shell of her left ear, winking mischievously in the waning sunlight. With her multihued skirt spread out around her in a kaleidoscope of colors, she was a gorgeous burst of color against a gray landscape.

Full of life and verve and authenticity he hadn't seen in a long time.

A thrilling sliver of excitement bloomed in his gut even as he frowned at the oversized stuffed teddy bear on the floor in front of her. Suddenly, the woman opened her mouth and screamed.

The cry was deep rather than shrill, perfectly modulated, and eerily familiar.

Vikram watched in increasing fascination as she extended her arms and bent to scoop up the stuffed toy from the ground into her arms. The gold and silver-colored bracelets she wore on one wrist tinkled at the moment, adding their own background score to the entire scene.

And then it came to him.

She *was* enacting a scene. From a recent movie. *His latest action thriller.*

She was…mocking him?

She was imitating the cheesiest line he'd ever said in front of a camera and she was doing a fantastic job of pinpointing everything he'd hated about the movie and in particular, that scene.

But instead of putting an end to what felt like a

mockery of his talent, his choices, and even him, Vikram continued to watch. Still curious to see what else she'd do. Bizarrely hungry for the spectacle the woman was making of him.

No wonder Virat was having the time of his life. In their recent argument, his younger brother hadn't packed his punches when he'd criticized that action thriller and every other career choice Vikram had made in the last fifteen years with the brilliant wit and rapacious tongue that he was famous for throughout the industry as a top Bollywood director.

It seemed his brother had been sitting on a mountain of complaints that had suddenly blown up in Vikram's face. The argument had begun after he'd confessed to Virat about his ridiculous proposal to Zara. Virat had unexpectedly gone ballistic about that, then moved on to an old disagreement about their sister Anya's future, then the script for a film Vikram had rejected last year…and finished with his brother calling him a control freak who just didn't know when to stop.

The woman hugged the imaginary person to her chest and bent her head, a low growl building out of her petite form. A couple of seconds passed as she buried her head in the stuffed toy's neck. Just as he'd done to the heroine in that scene. Even the theater hadn't had this kind of pin-drop silence from the audience that she did.

His chest burned with embarrassment, even the beginnings of anger but there was something else too. He continued to watch, as captivated as the rest of them.

The low growl erupted from the woman's throat as she let the huge toy roll away from her lap and, in a movement that was creepily close to his own movements, she raised her head, pushed her fingers to the back of her neck, and screamed again in simulated fury and anguish.

She managed to pitch her voice pretty low, sounding almost as a man might. And then, she looked up.

"I will avenge you, Meri Jaan, in this life and the next. I will destroy everyone that harmed you. I will paint the world with the blood of the man that wronged you. I am the destroyer."

The wretched woman even started humming the soundtrack that followed those horrible lines of dialogue. Who was she?

Applause broke around her. With a familiarity that Vikram found annoying on a disproportionate level, Virat wrapped his arm around the woman and pulled her into a hug against him. Even Daadi laughed.

And then it clicked. This was his grandmother's new personal assistant. The wonderful Ms. Naina Menon that Daadi couldn't stop singing praises of. The one who'd been hired by his grandmother around two months ago, after she'd done some work for Virat. Vikram had never met her.

"You could give most of the leading ladies a run for their money, darling," said Virat.

She shook her head. "Thanks, Virat. But I'm not made for acting. I...this was just—"

Pushing his hands into the pockets of his trousers, Vikram stepped into the room. "My brother's right, Ms. Menon."

The cheerful atmosphere died an instant death. The servants disappeared like rats at the sight of a big cat. Slender fingers pushing away at her unruly cloud of hair in a nervous gesture, the woman turned to face him.

Large, wide eyes alighted on his face, and there was a tremble to that pink mouth. "Hello, Mr. Raawal. I can't tell you how excited I am to finally meet you." It should have sounded pandering, syrupy, and yet the sentiment in her words was clearly genuine.

The fascination he'd felt as he'd taken in her plump curves morphed into a rumbling growl inside his chest, not unlike the one she'd just done in imitation of him. "I wish I could say the same of you, Ms. Menon," he said, his tone betraying nothing but icy disdain.

"I'm sorry if that performance offended you, Mr. Raawal. It was meant to just be a bit of fun…" She looked incredibly young as she visibly swallowed. "I wasn't mocking you."

"No? It sounded like you were," he retorted softly, childishly put out that he was Mr. Raawal while his brother was Virat. Of course, Virat had been charming women since he'd been in *langotis*, so it wasn't much of a surprise. "You *are* wasting your talents here. If not the silver screen, you should be on one of those talk shows, making money from doing the caustic commentaries that are all the rage now, mocking every artist, and bringing them down for the world's glee."

The moment the words were out of his mouth,

Vikram regretted them. Even before he noticed her stricken expression. He'd been called arrogant, blunt, even grumpy, but never cruel, not even by the media that kept looking for dirt underneath the shield of his public persona.

But that had been downright cruel.

She went from laughing and glowing to a pinched paleness that punched a hole in his bitterness.

Virat interrupted. "*Bhai*, Daadi and I insisted that she—"

"What do you do with that talent?" he cut in, once again disproportionately riled by Virat's protective stance toward this relative stranger. For some reason, Vikram was far too invested in this woman's opinion of him.

Ms. Menon continued to stare up at him, big eyes wide, tension swathing her petite frame. He moved closer to her and felt that tug again. She was pretty in a girl-next-door way, but the expression in those eyes, the rapid change from anger to desire to confusion…it made her utterly gorgeous.

God, she only looked about twenty.

"Lost your ability for words now?" he murmured, more to hear her speak again than anything else.

She glared at him. "I don't understand your question."

"You're clearly talented, Ms. Menon. What do you do with it all? I mean, other than making a mockery of others?"

"I was… I was just showing them my mimicry. I even did a few other actors earlier too. Like Big B."

"Ahh…so you're one of those critics who makes

fun but has never done a minute's worth of creative work themselves or shared it with the world? It's so easy to hide on the sidelines and mock the person out in the public arena, no? Can I ask why you pinpointed that particular scene?"

Her spine straightened and she charged forward. The scent of roses filled his nostrils and he felt a thrill run down his spine. God, she was gorgeous when she was all riled up.

"First of all, I'm not ill-equipped to make such comments. Not when I've studied film history all through college. Secondly, are you sure you want to know why I picked that scene to reenact?"

"I'm a big boy, Ms. Menon. I assure you I can take it."

"Can you though? When you've turned a minute of comedy into a huge insult to your own ego?" He didn't answer and the resolve tightened in her face. "Fine, here's my honest opinion, for what it's worth.

"You cater to the lowest denomination of the mass population with these action blockbusters, and you offer a warped image of what a hero should be with your revenge and destroy plotlines. You perpetuate the same tired old trope of being the macho guy who's a 'true man' just because you can supposedly beat up more guys than anyone else. That movie was not only gratuitously violent but offensive on every level to women, from your leading lady to your blind sister to even your overdramatized female best friend. They only exist in the film to make you their savior."

Every word of her criticism was justified. Every word was utter truth.

And he'd asked for it, so he couldn't even blame her for saying it, could he?

If Vikram didn't hate the idea of true physical violence on every level, he would've sucker-punched his brother for the low whistle that ran around the room.

"I make movies to make money, Ms. Menon. Having clearly inveigled yourself into my grandmother's household, I'm sure you've a really good idea that it's wealth which makes the world go around. So please don't tell me that all artists create just for the purpose of art."

He had no idea why he'd just said that because his grandmother was a great judge of character. And if she thought Ms. Menon was the newly rising sun, then Vikram would normally have believed her, no questions asked.

"Inveigled myself?" she repeated in a low tone, her body vibrating with her anger. "I can't... I can't believe I used to have a teenage crush on you! Of course, I know wealth makes the world go around probably far better than you do—because, believe me, I don't have any.

"As for art... I'm not asking you to throw away any of your considerable wealth making artsy movies that might bomb at the box office. I know you have to keep growing this amazing dynasty..." she threw her arms around and those damn bracelets of hers tinkled again "...to enable the generations of Raawals that might come after you to sit around on their bums."

She slapped her hand over her mouth and groaned. Vikram felt the insane urge to drag her hand away and taste that groan. As much as she was skewering him with her painful truths, he wanted to hear her go on tirade after tirade. God, he could listen to that throaty voice of hers for hours.

She turned to address his grandmother. "I'm sorry, Daadiji. I didn't mean to insult your family."

Virat and Daadi laughed and even Vikram's chest filled with a burst of irreverent joy.

"Never mind, *beta*," Daadi crooned, her perceptive gaze on Vikram. "No one else would dare rip into my grandson quite so well as you just have. Please go on. You have my blessing." The last he knew was added for his benefit.

Not that she believed he would harm Ms. Menon in any way.

"I don't think she has the guts, Daadi," Vikram taunted deliberately. "She's too scared to say anything else to my face."

Fury coated her cheeks, and her brown eyes danced with fire.

"You're not just wealthy, you wield power and influence. Directors and producers change story lines for you. They hire and fire people at your say-so. They create these multi-crore elaborate sets for you. You have the chance to steer things the right way in the industry. You could use your star power to create a new kind of hero, Mr. Raawal. Because, believe me, the world needs to reexamine what makes a man a hero."

Vikram knew he should leave it at that. She hadn't

said anything he hadn't already faced up to in the dark of the night. And yet to be so thoroughly reduced to the sum of his flaws grated at his ego. To be thought of in such poor terms by a woman that stirred his interest like never before…pricked his male pride.

"Why should I give your cutting opinion any weight? What have you done so far that's so important and worthwhile? You're clearly both educated and talented because even Virat sings your praises, and yet you're hiding here playing PA to my grandmother, hiding from your own life!"

"That's unfair," she threw back at him and yet he could see from her reaction he'd hit the nail on its head. He hadn't become the king of an industry without being perceptive.

"Ah… Ms. Menon, you can dish it out, but you clearly can't take it," he drawled.

"You don't know anything about my life," she retorted and he had a horrible feeling he'd truly wounded her.

Regret filled his chest. He desperately wanted to touch her, to hold her trembling body. Instead he stepped back.

For the entire world, even for his family who knew him well, he was a coldhearted businessman, the head of Raawal House. And nothing else. With no shades or flaws.

"And yet you presume to know everything about mine," he said softly, his frustration with himself, with the world seeping into his tone. "Because I live my life for your entertainment and God forbid I make mistakes like every other person on the planet. God forbid anyone even wonders that there's more to me than the company or this bloody family or being a successful star. Right?"

Silence met his own outburst. Virat and Daadi stared at him with stunned expressions. As for Ms. Menon, he had no words to describe the look in her eyes.

It wasn't pity or sympathy. It was something else, something he wanted to drown in. Something he wanted to demand she give voice to.

Which was crazy enough in itself.

Vikram turned around and walked away from the damned woman with her far-too-blunt opinions and big eyes and from the house with its insistent mockery of what he should've been and what he had become instead.

Damn it, how had the woman gotten under his skin so easily? Why had it taken someone like her to point out the obvious truth of how far off course he'd veered? To make him suddenly understand the reason for his recent burnout?

Because he'd surrounded himself with yes-men and women. Because he'd made himself so powerful, so untouchable that there wasn't anyone who would dare dig into him like she just had. Except Virat. And he hadn't really listened to his brother.

Because in the pursuit of trying to fix everything their father had destroyed, he'd sold his soul in the process.

CHAPTER TWO

"YOU'RE HIDING HERE..."

One bitingly truthful comment from Vikram Raawal had been enough to make Naina ache to take action. One small tidbit of gossip from her stepsister, Maya, that Naina's ex was getting engaged had propelled her into doing this...

And now she was here. At a masked ball in borrowed glad rags, determined to have fun. The minute Naina had asked him, Virat had agreed to bring her to his parents' latest charity ball, a mischievous smile lighting up his entire face. He'd always been friendly, charming but since her tirade at his older brother, he'd positively showered her with affection.

They'd arrived not two hours ago, waved in through the high gates into a beautiful winding pathway toward yet another bungalow the Raawals owned.

Naina took a glass of some frothy pink cocktail as she moved around the dance floor in the expansive ballroom.

Her eyes were going to be permanently stuck in

a wide-eyed position from all the celebrities she had spotted so far. Even with elaborate, custom-designed, gem-encrusted masks, the stunning features of more than one actor and beautiful actress were obvious. And yet, there was a strange thrill in the air as most of the A-listers pretended as if they didn't know each other.

Was that the attraction of a masquerade ball? Were these people so jaded that a pretend dress-up party passed for excitement in their frenetic, under-the-microscope lives?

Looking like one of them, even if every inch of her had been pinched, pushed, molded, painted, had been much easier than she'd imagined. Especially since Daadiji had tasked an entire team to dress Naina for the party.

The baby-pink A-line dress in chiffon, one of Anya Raawal's own creations, had initially reminded Naina of a birthday frock her stepmother, Jaya Ma, had bought her when she'd been twelve. Full of layers and gauzy material, that frock had made Naina look like pink bubblegum. But since the elegant Ms. Raawal had been doing Naina a favor with this dress, she'd kept her mouth shut.

Once she had stood in front of the full-length mirror, Naina had quickly realized that Anya was a genius. The dress hugged her body from chest to waist and then flared wide, making the most of her short stature. With her unruly hair straightened to within an inch of its life, it fell to her waist in a long silky curtain.

With her hair not stealing the focus from her face and with cleverly applied makeup, her eyes seemed huge in her face. Even Naina had thought she looked almost beautiful.

After two dances and an introduction to one of her favorite writers, she'd insisted that Virat do his own thing. She'd realized from Daadiji's sharp surprise he was even attending this party, that Virat usually gave a wide berth to anything related to his parents.

"I feel like I'm releasing an innocent doe into a horde of stampeding beasts," Virat had said when she'd demanded if he was going to stick to her like last week's gum.

"If you stand by me the entire time, shooting glares at any man who even looks at me," she said with a smile, "I might as well freeze in place and look like one of these priceless sculptures that are dotted around. Please, Virat. I'm not as helpless as I look."

That had done it.

She'd kissed him on the cheek, nodded obediently when he gave her strict instructions to text him when she was ready to leave, and then he disappeared into the crowd.

For the next half hour, Naina stayed on the steps going out into the balmy night, standing on the fringes of a group, listening to them argue the finer points of why remake mania had taken over the industry.

"You're hiding, Ms. Menon," said a deep voice in her head and she took a long drink of her cocktail in

defiance. Damn Vikram Raawal. She wasn't going to let the man have the last word.

Spotting another young actor that she thought was particularly cute, Naina edged along the perimeter of the dancing crowd, determined to introduce herself.

It wasn't until an hour and a half later when Naina reached the huge library and closed the door behind her that she took in a deep breath. The last thing she wanted was another confrontation with Vikram Raawal.

No matter that he stood so separate from the crowd at the party, almost as if he was as out of place among these people as she herself. Which was ridiculous.

For one dazzling second, their eyes had met across the room, the rhythmic beat of the music around them in concert with her own heart. For one insane second, Naina had felt as if he'd actually seen her. The real her.

The usually dull, plump, bookish Naina Menon who stood on the sidelines and watched life pass her by. It felt as if he'd known that it was she beneath the mask.

Luckily, his attention had been quickly drawn away by a costar of his. And whatever spell, imagined or real, had woven between them, had been broken.

"And yet you presume to know everything about me..." Those words of his haunted her.

He had been right. Who was she to moralize to

anyone else? She had not only criticized him, but she had attacked his worth as a person.

Naina sat down on a comfortable lounger and pulled her cell phone out of her clutch to text Virat. She'd had enough of the party and the loud music.

She had introduced herself to a lot of people, she'd danced, she'd shamelessly fan-girled over one Urdu poet that Papa and she had adored for years by reciting his own poem back at him, she had laughed at the not-so-funny joke by an actor who had been called the latest wonder boy to breeze into the industry. The same one she'd thought was cute.

For all his gorgeous features and ripped body, Naina had found him deeply boring. Really, the man-child had talked about himself—his workout regimen, his Instagram followers, the love letters he received from his rabid, female fans professing undying love to his perfectly chiseled abdomen—for more than half an hour. Without saying anything of significance concerning the arts or films or theater or anything.

Holding her arm up, she moved her phone around to get a signal. She was about to go find Virat in person when the huge double doors of the library opened. And in walked *the very man* she'd wanted to avoid, not just for tonight, not just this week, but for the rest of her life.

Vikram hadn't noticed her yet. She'd turned off most of the lights, leaving only the dim lamp next to her switched on. Not until he reached the pool of soft light thrown by the lamp did he see her.

"I didn't realize anyone else needed to escape that madness," he said after a beat of silence. In the near dark, his voice sounded impossibly deep, sliding over her skin like a note of music.

She didn't answer. She couldn't. Couldn't find the words past her dry mouth and the rapid drumbeat of her heart in her ears.

"Are you all right?" he asked, concern filling his voice.

Naina took a deep breath and pitched her voice lower than usual. "I am. Thank you. I just…"

"You were clearly not enjoying the party."

"I was. I mean, I am. How do you know, anyway?"

"I was watching you in the other room." He raised his hands and backed up a step when she frowned. "In a non-creepy way, that is. There's something very familiar about you and I was trying to remember if we had met."

Heat poured into Naina's cheeks and she ducked her head. That feeling of being consumed by his gaze returned. She looked up to find him studying her intently and she was immensely grateful she'd kept her mask on when she'd walked into the library. "No. I don't know you." She smiled at her own words. "I mean I *do* know who you are."

She pointed a finger at his unmasked face. He was wearing a white shirt, unbuttoned at his throat, his hair a little bit on the longer side right now. The subdued light from the lamp only served to highlight the beautiful symmetry of his features. "I wondered why you clearly touted the rules of the party. But then I realized you'd have been recognized even with a mask on. Your face is certainly perfect enough," she blurted out and then instantly regretted it. "I'm sorry. I didn't mean to push myself and my compliments into your space. I've learned recently how much I presume…" She cleared her throat and looked away. "Sorry."

"Since I was the one who intruded on your solitude, shall we call a truce?"

She nodded.

"May I sit down?"

"Yes, but it's literally your parents' house. I should be the one to—"

"No, please stay. That way, we can be alone together. Instead of being forced to socialize."

Her suddenly teenaged heart went pitter-patter at that. "Why are you hiding?"

"I usually come to these parties just to keep an eye on…things." He folded his tall, lean form next to her with movements that were sheer poetry in motion. "I promised my brother I'd give his friend a lift home. He had to leave suddenly."

She straightened instantly. "Wait, Virat already left? But he said…" She flushed furiously when he saw Vikram studying her with a raised brow.

"Ah…that's why you were waiting for him here? In the dark. In secret. You should know, Virat is notorious for changing his girlfriends as easily as he changes actors for his projects."

"What?"

"He left with that new pop singer."

There was a strange gentleness in his voice that enveloped her. "Why are you telling me that?"

"It's better to cut your losses now rather than have your heart trampled later on by Virat. He's ditched you and whatever exciting, private tryst you'd both planned and gone home with another woman."

Naina looked around the quiet, shady nook she'd chosen in the vast library, the rest of which was enveloped in darkness. "You think I was waiting here to meet Virat so that we could…for some secret… to have a private…" The longer she stumbled over her words, the more she blushed and the wider the dratted man's smile grew.

"Virat is well known for his…adventurous exploits."

"I'm not waiting here for your brother so that we can get it on in some kind of secret, silly seduction game."

"No?"

"No. And stop smirking at me in that condescending way."

His mouth straightened but the smile lingered in his eyes. *Gorgeous* did not do the man justice. "I'm not smirking or condescending. I just find you adorable."

"I'm no such thing and how…what?" Apparently, the night was full of surprises.

"You apologized for invading my personal space and for complimenting my perfect features. You're trying very hard to sound all sophisticated about men and seduction yet it's clear you're not, and the effect is very endearing."

"My ex did say I was far too old-fashioned." Naina sighed. The temptation to pull off the mask was overwhelming but it meant whatever this camaraderie between them was…would disappear in a breath.

It was strange how life worked. She had covered her face with a mask because she wanted to be someone else for one night. And yet, even with the mask in place, she felt seen for the first time in a long time. By the very man she'd torn into not a few days ago for his insensitive portrayal of women.

If he realized who she was, there was no doubt he'd walk away without a backward glance. He might even think she'd…*tricked* him. She couldn't bear the thought of tonight ending like that, the thought of him thinking ill of her.

She wanted more from tonight. From him. From herself.

"Are you old-fashioned?"

Naina shrugged. "What does that even mean? Who decides what's modern and what's old-fashioned anyway? And why are all those stupid, arbitrary constructs only applied to women? You and Virat are praised as playboys whereas every move your sister Anya makes is held to some vague standards of behavior no one else in your family is held accountable to."

"Ah…now I know how you became close to my brother." His arm went around the chaise lounge. "Also, your ex sounds like a jackass who wanted to push you into things you were not ready for. And because he's probably a mama's boy used to getting what he wants, he attached a label to you to make you feel bad about it. You should be glad you dumped his ass."

"I didn't. He dumped me," Naina replied automatically, stunned to her core at this seemingly arrogant man's astute summary of Rohan. Hadn't Jaya Ma always said the same? Why hadn't Naina seen it? Why had she let him hurt her like that?

She looked at Vikram with new eyes.

"Then I'd suggest you be thankful for whatever brought that around."

"He had started a new job in Delhi last year, and asked me to move in with him. First Papa got really sick, so I had to postpone it. Then after Papa died, we discovered we were up to our neck in debt. So my ex decided he didn't want to be held back any longer by my dead weight. He had places to go, careers to achieve."

Thankfully, he didn't offer any meaningless platitudes to fill up the silence like Maya had or say *I told you so* like Jaya Ma. He simply honored her feelings of grief and betrayal. Naina didn't know how long they sat quietly like that. But she absolutely knew she liked being alone together with him.

"He's not a bad guy really," she finally said into the silence.

He snorted. She glared at him.

"So if you were not waiting for Virat for a secret seduction, what did you want with him?"

"Oh, he…he was only supposed to give me a lift

back home, that's all. I'd had enough of my wild crazy night. Did he really dump me onto you to take home?"

He shrugged. "Virat has a weird sense of humor. Was the party everything you imagined it might be?"

"I... I wanted excitement and drama. And I certainly got more than enough to last me for a decade."

"I saw you dance earlier with that hot young actor. I tried to keep an eye on you but I got distracted. He didn't act...inappropriately with you, did he?"

Naina colored at his direct question. "Oh, no, nothing like that. I got the impression that I was far too beneath his usual standards to be the object of his lust. The dance he indulged me with was, I believe, his charity act for the year. Maybe for the decade."

Those beautiful brown eyes of his swept over her face as if taking inventory. Naina felt as if he had actually touched her. "Charity act?"

"Apparently, he doesn't date anyone who's not at least eight inches taller and twenty kilos lighter than me. Or alternately a few crores richer than I am.

"But he decided he could be generous enough to give me a taste of how it felt to be in his arms. A treat to remember when I return to my unglamorous, unhappening life, as he put it. God save me from men who want to save me from my apparently pitiful existence!"

Laughter burst from him so suddenly that Naina startled.

She pushed back into the lounger until her legs were crossed away from his and she could study this gorgeous man with his stunning smile. All evening, she'd thought whatever magical quality she'd been chasing tonight had been nonexistent. That she was foolish to have expected life to be more exciting just because she'd entered a different world for a few hours.

But sitting here with Vikram, and seeing his irreverent smile and knowing that she'd caused it, this was the magic she'd been looking for. This moment, with its explosive, exciting possibilities.

"I'm glad my life is a source of entertainment to you, Mr. Raawal."

"Vikram." A simple command.

She shook her head. "I won't know you long enough to be so presumptuous."

"Try," he urged, with a half smile around his mouth, and she found herself nodding. If he smiled like that and asked her to follow him into hell, Naina had a feeling she would do it without a blink.

Was that why so many women—actresses and models and businesswomen alike—fell for him year after year, even knowing that he would never commit to any of them? In-depth details of his love life, if it existed, never graced any magazine or TV channel. Only frequent speculations about his relationship with actress Zara Khan—which by its long-standing nature made the media hungry for more.

"I'm sorry your exciting evening turned out to be…exhausting."

"It isn't a complete waste." She ran her palms over the soft chiffon of her dress and smiled. "I got to dress up and play a star for one evening. I danced with more than one gorgeous stud, I saw things that I never thought I would. I met Husainji, although I'm afraid I made a fool of myself by reciting his own poem back at him. Papa would have loved to be here. For that alone, I'm happy I came tonight."

He smiled.

"And I got to look beautiful for one night."

"I have a feeling you look beautiful whatever you're wearing, Ms...."

False names came and went from Naina's lips. "Please don't ask me to tell you my identity. I don't want to return to the real world just yet."

"Tell me why you came tonight then."

"I just heard that my ex is engaged to be married. He...found a girlfriend a mere month after he dumped me and now she's his fiancée. The other night, I got into an argument with...someone and what they said, it really shook me. I took a good look at my life, at myself, and I just... I became angry with myself.

"Since Papa died, I've been flitting from job to job, situation to situation, letting circumstances and other people push me around. For one night, I wanted to be in control. I wanted to...not be in control too. I just didn't want to be the boring N...girl that people left behind."

Something shimmered in his eyes, something that looked like desire. But no, that wasn't possible. This man, this gorgeous superstar couldn't be attracted to her. For all the makeup and the dress and the glittering mask, she was still only Naina.

Naina Menon, whose sole accomplishment so far had been running away from her own life. Despite the smiles and down-to-earth attitude of his, Vikram was used to seeing perfection from sunup to sundown.

"I'm sorry," she said, looking away. "I don't think I'm making much sense."

His hand reached for hers on the back of the sofa, barely touching the tips of her fingers. The slight contact was teasing, yet grounding. As if he saw her clearly even in the darkness. "You're making perfect sense.

"I'd give anything to not be Vikram Raawal for one day. To forget that my every breath, every look, every step is hounded by the media. To make mistakes like any other man and not be vilified for it. To throw off the shackles of..." He looked away, his fingers roughly thrusting through his hair. A laugh, full of self-mockery burst from his mouth. "God, you're a dangerous woman. And believe me, I have known enough of them."

Her smile faltered and he instantly caught it. "What have I said wrong?"

"I don't like the way you lump women together, as if we all share the same brain. The same thoughts. Have the same agenda."

"That's the second time this week I've been criticized by someone for my bias against women." He rubbed a hand over his face, as if he was truly tired.

"As galling as it is to admit, I owe both of you an apology," he said, stealing away the ground from under her feet.

Another teasing smile. "Now you're shocked that I even know the meaning of the word."

"No, I just…"

"It's okay. Even with that mask on, you have the most expressive face I've ever seen. Your eyes flash like glittering gems when you're angry and your mouth…" His gaze dipped to it and a flash of electricity seemed to strike them both simultaneously.

Suddenly depleting the air from the room. Filling her skin with a restless energy. Filling her mind with impossibly wanton desires that could never come true.

Dreams and desires that had to be impossible, didn't they? She wasn't actually thinking of kissing Vikram Raawal, was she? She couldn't.

"You've got that feverish glint in your eyes again. Tell me what you're thinking."

"That this day couldn't get any more bizarre. That I had no idea what I'd signed up for. That wanting to kiss you has to be the most impossible thought to ever cross my mind."

He didn't flinch at her statement. He didn't even blink. He just sat there and stared at her with those eyes that seemed to devour her.

Naina could feel her cheeks burning. Mortification, she'd tell Maya, had a special kind of sting. If only the earth could burst open like it did so often in his blockbusters and swallow her whole. Closing her eyes didn't change reality. He was still there, solid as ever, watching her.

It caused fast words to spill out of her without her permission. "I don't know what just got into me. I'm thoroughly ashamed of myself and not that this makes it any better, but believe me, my desire to kiss you doesn't arise from the fact that you're *the* Vikram Raawal, Bollywood superstar, eligible bachelor and one of the wealthiest men in the country."

"No?" he said.

He didn't sound accusatory. It encouraged her to carry on.

"No. I mean, I know I can't just isolate the movie star part of you, but that's not the draw for me," Naina clarified breathlessly. She didn't know why it mattered so much that he believed her. That she wasn't some mindless groupie that wanted to live out a kind of warped fantasy here.

"Tell me what it is then?"

His question had a curious thirst to it. As if he desperately wanted to know why she wanted him. As if hearing a woman's admiration for him wasn't a regular thing in his world, only she knew that it was.

"I want to kiss the man that saw me across the room this evening. The man that can laugh at himself, who is maybe just as lonely as I've been, for all that he has the world at his feet. The complicated stranger with whom I've found a connection in a quiet, darkened room made for secret trysts," she finished with a smile, loving this fearless version of herself.

Their gazes held, a live wire of electricity sparking into life between them.

For a long time, he didn't say anything. And Naina was okay with that too. He had given her something tonight, something precious. Self-confidence. And she wanted to give something back to him, this man who had everything in the world.

"Then come kiss me. I'm all yours."

Her heart went thud against her rib cage. "What?"

"Kiss me," he repeated and as if to underscore his invitation, he spread his legs apart, making room for her. "Have your way with me. Do with me whatever you will."

Naina had never felt more terrified and more thrilled in her entire life. Not even when Papa had taken her and Mama to see snow for the first time when she'd been six and they'd stood at the top of a snow-covered mountain, both majestic and terrifying in its presence.

"Why?" she managed to ask, trying to cling to the last remnants of any sanity that might be left.

"Shall I speak my mind? I'll probably be blunt."

"You're a gentleman to ask permission. I believe I crossed that line long ago."

"I want to see if that lovely mouth of yours tastes as good as it looks. I want to tear that mask and that dress off and touch every inch of you. I want to cover those gorgeous breasts with my hands and mouth until you're begging me for more. I want to be inside you while you laugh with your beautiful eyes and strip another layer of clothing off me."

"Oh." Her clutch slipped from Naina's hands, falling onto the floor in a sinuous whisper. "Why?"

He sighed. "Because when a man thinks a woman is incredibly sexy, he wants to do things to her. With her. Wild, wicked things. He wants to—"

"I said I don't have much experience, not that I'm lacking basic common sense," Naina interrupted, feeling a tingle of excitement all over her skin. The chiffon suddenly felt like a tight cage against it.

He smiled and shrugged. "I warned you I'd be blunt."

It was the kind of smile that made girls like her put posters of him up on their walls after his debut movie. There was charm and mischief in that smile. She hadn't seen it that day at his grandmother's house. A little glow erupted in her chest that she'd made him smile like that again. As if it were a prize to be won.

"Honesty seems to be the best policy when you want to do all those things with someone," she agreed and again, he laughed.

Naina felt as if she was the richest person in the world. She wanted to spend entire eons making him laugh like this. While he whispered filthy things in her ear and made her damp between her legs.

"Says the woman who won't reveal who she is."

"If I reveal myself, I can't be this wild, crazy woman."

"But I have to call you something." He swept his gaze over her with a scorching intensity that put paid to any doubts she harbored. "I've got it. Dream Girl."

She laughed. "That name is for beautiful divas like Hema Malini," she said, naming the star of the seventies who'd taken both the industry and her leading men by storm. There was even a song with that title.

"It suits you just as well it suited her." He shook his head when she'd have protested. The moment stretched and she finally nodded, taking the compliment with a grace she didn't usually possess. "You don't feel it? This thing between us?"

"I do. Absolutely." She had felt the tension between them even the other day. When they'd been busy lobbing verbal grenades at each other. "But I…" She licked her mouth and his gaze immediately focused there. "I'm not good at reading the signals. I didn't want to assume that you'd be attracted to someone like me."

"Ah…who's stereotyping now?"

"There's a certain truth to stereotyping," she protested, feeling flustered.

"In yours but not in mine?" he said gently, calling her out.

"It's just that… I'm not what you call conventionally beautiful. Please, I'm not asking for compliments. And I'm fully aware that conventional beauty is also an arbitrary standard. It's just that you're used to being with incredibly sophisticated, beautiful, accomplished women. Like we established earlier, I'm little more than a novice when it comes to men and their desires."

"I've definitely never met a woman who disagreed with me so much."

A shaft of joy blew through Naina. She loved how he made her smile. Even when she was mostly attacking him. "I couldn't bear it if you were laughing at me. Or worse, condescending to me like that arrogant young stud earlier."

"You think I'm asking you to kiss me out of some sense of pity?"

"If not pity, at least as an experiment."

"Every kiss is an experiment. Sometimes, the result is that whatever chemistry you had burning between you just fizzled out. Sometimes, you find that flame in the strangest of places with the last person you'd have ever thought of."

"See? Because I'm not your type."

"No, because I don't know you. Not even your name. Should I tell you the risk I'm taking right now?"

Naina snorted inelegantly. "There's nothing you risk by indulging the silly woman who wants to kiss you senseless. Who wants to muss you up so thoroughly with her hands that she's shaking. Who wants to…" She trailed off at the unholy glint of wickedness in his eyes, then swallowed and found the courage to continue. "Press her mouth against the hollow at your throat and make you feel as crazy as she does."

"Kiss me senseless… Ahh…love, now you're just winding me up." He smiled, his teeth digging into his lower lip, grooves in his cheeks and a dark twinkle in his eyes. Energy vibrated from his frame. As if he was thoroughly excited at the thought of her kissing him senseless. "If you could see yourself as I see you right now, threatening all kinds of delicious sensual attacks on me…"

Anticipation licked through her body, releasing a restless hunger. "Tell me, what great risk are you taking right now?"

"You know who I am. You know pretty much everything about me. My favorite color, my favorite car, my favorite dish, probably even my favorite position with a partner." He sounded close to disgusted, and Naina realized he was right. What she was doing was not a risk at all. Not when compared to him. "Tomorrow morning, you could go to any media outlet you want and tell them all about this moment. You could repeat everything I said to you tonight. You could sell this story and probably make enough money to last the rest of your life."

Naina vibrated with anger and hurt. "I would never do that. Ever. Revealing to anyone what might happen between you and me tonight would be a total betrayal of myself."

Those long fingers of his slid against hers until they were entwined. His touch sent a jolt of warmth up her arm. "I believe you. You've no idea how fantastic that is."

"How?"

He sighed. "I am Vikram Raawal. From the moment I could understand the world, it meant something. It meant more to other people even before I understood what it meant to me. Privilege and power and pride, yes. But so much more that the world doesn't see. Everybody wants something from me. My family, my friends, my fans…apparently even my critics. There are so many expectations that they feel like shackles around my ankles."

He pressed a finger against her mouth when she opened it. "Hear me out before you give me another speech about my civic duties, please. I'm more than happy to lend a word or a hand when I can. But it's not every day that someone comes to me with no expectations of me. Expect maybe what my mouth can do for her."

Naina let her gaze fall to study it. "It *is* a gorgeous mouth," she whispered on a long sigh and it came again.

His laughter. Deep and rumbling. Turning his face into a thing of beauty. That need between them shimmered into life again, gaining in intensity, until it was a peal ringing deep inside her body. He tugged and she scooted closer to him on the sofa. The warmth of his body was a tempting caress against her bare arms.

"I want to join you in your fantasy and escape. So for tonight, I'm all yours, Dream Girl."

"I can muss you up however I want?" Naina asked, stunned by her own daring.

Again, he dug those teeth into his lower lip and nodded.

"I can take this however far I want?"

"Yes."

"And if I…"

"If you want to stop, we will stop. This is absolutely your show, baby. In fact, how about I don't touch you unless you ask me to?"

"I was going to say what if I don't know what to do next?" she murmured.

"Then you can ask me to help you along."

Her heart beating a million to the dozen, Naina covered the small distance that still remained between them. It was akin to flying off a cliff. But she wanted this kiss. She wanted this man, so she took a deep breath and shoved herself off the edge.

CHAPTER THREE

SHE HAD THE silkiest-looking skin Vikram had ever seen. And as he'd said, he'd seen a number of stunning women during his career. There was a glow, a suppleness to it that he knew no amount of makeup could achieve. It made him want to lift his hand and stroke his knuckles softly down one cheek. It made him want to nuzzle his nose into the hollow underneath her ear and test for himself if she was also that silky to the touch.

Eyes wide, breathing shallow, she shuffled herself toward him slowly, carefully.

The scent of her hit him first. A subtle blend of jasmine and her that he'd remember for the rest of his life. And equate with honesty and irreverence and passion and laughter. There was a joy about this woman, despite her insecurities and vulnerabilities, that he found almost magical.

The mask she wore was black satin with elaborate gold threading at the edges and was woven tightly into her hair, leaving just enough of her beautiful dark brown eyes visible. The bridge of her small nose was revealed as was the slice of her cheekbones. For a few seconds, Vikram had the overwhelming urge to tear it off. He wanted to see her face. Not because he wanted to find out her identity.

He wanted to see her face because he wanted to know this woman. He wanted to know everything about her. He wanted... With a rueful shake of his head, he pushed away the urge. It was more than clear that men had only ever disappointed her. He was damned if he was going to be counted as one of them. He wanted to be different in her memory.

When she remembered him after tonight, he wanted her to smile. He wanted her to crave more of him. Just as he would crave more of her. He knew this before their lips even touched. And he would find a way to discover her identity. He was just as sure of that too.

Her mouth was completely uncovered. Her lipstick was mostly gone leaving a faint pink smudge that he wanted to lick away with his tongue. He was already half-hard and he hadn't even touched her. Or been touched. He hadn't felt this excited at the prospect of a simple kiss in so long. Not since he'd been a boy.

She held the edge of her silk dress with one hand and as she'd lifted it to move, he got a flash of a thigh. Soft and smooth and silky. It was like receiving a jolt of electricity, with every inch he discovered of this woman. The dress swooped low in the front, baring the upper curves of her breasts in a tantalizing display.

He wanted to lick the line of her cleavage until she was panting against him. He wanted to sneak his hand under that neckline and push her breasts out until he could uncover the tight knots of her nipples that were thrusting against the silk now.

And then there she was, within touching distance. Sitting with her legs folded beneath her, looking straight into his eyes. One arm held the sofa while the other smoothed repeatedly over the slight curve of her belly. She was nervous and he found it both endearing and incredibly arousing. She wanted to please herself. And him. And he'd never wanted more for a woman to discover pleasure with him.

Her warm breath hit him somewhere between his mouth and jaw in silky strokes that resonated with his heartbeat. This close, he could see the tiny scar on the other corner of her mouth.

"Are you going to do anything?" she asked after a couple of seconds, sounding completely put out.

He wanted to laugh and tug that pouty lower lip with his teeth. Instead he forced himself to take a breath. He was never going to smell jasmine and not think of her ever again. "It's your kiss, darling. You take it."

She looked at him as if he was her favorite experiment. "Okay, here goes," she whispered, her brow knotting in concentration.

His breath hitching in his throat, Vikram waited. Small hands cradled his jaw and cheek and then there she was, leaning forward. Pressing those lovely lips against his. Soft and tentative and incredibly lush against his mouth. Warm and smelling of mint and sherbet. A quick slanted press. Then another. A quiet drag of that wide mouth, this way and that. A tentative flick of her tongue against the seam of his lips. An exhale that played his nerve endings like the strokes of a piano. And then she pulled back.

She stroked his lips with a featherlight touch. "You're not participating," she protested.

"Say my name."

She frowned and sighed. And mumbled something to herself. Something like "If you want to do anything properly, you have to do it yourself."

He chuckled.

The minx pressed her palm to his chest. His heart thundered away at her touch. Her gaze intent, she moved the hand down to his abdomen. And then lower, until her fingertips rested against the waistband of his trousers.

A burst of strange sensation erupted around his heart and he groaned. She studied their bodies some more, as if it was as complex as rocket science. He wondered if she was just plain torturing him. But no, clearly, the woman didn't have a manipulative bone in her body.

It was the hardest thing he'd ever done to sit still. When all he wanted was to push her down onto the sofa and show her what kissing someone senseless really meant. He wanted to cover her luscious body with his, lick his way into that tart mouth and grind his growing erection into the cradle of her legs. "Do you need help?" he asked and barely recognized his own voice.

Her head jerked up, her fingers still pressing against his lips. He licked the tip of one that was peeking into his mouth. And then nipped it gently with his teeth. "What was that for?" she gasped.

He shrugged. "You have thirty seconds to act, Dream Girl."

"If not?"

"If not, I simply get up and walk away."

"You're a cruel, cruel man, Vikram Raawal. And no, I won't let you walk away. Not yet."

Her weight shifted forward. A graze of those gorgeous full breasts against his chest. The tips of her fingers dug into his abdomen for purchase when she slipped slightly. She frowned some more. With a curse, she lifted the hem of her dress. Flashed her toned thighs at him and blushed furiously. And then she was straddling his legs, the soft curves of her body leaning forward at an angle and pressing against his in a completely delicious torture. He went from half-mast to fully hard in an instant.

"You know," she said, between humming a tune against his cheek, tracing every inch of his face with that mouth, "Papa used to say, if you do something, you should do it right." She opened her mouth and continued her foray, up one cheek, down the other, his neck, and then back up, leaving little pockets of warmth on his skin. Leaving him panting for more.

Vikram wondered if she could hear the hard thud of his heart. And then she was kissing him properly.

Hot and hard and honest. Like thunder on a stormy evening. Like the earthy scent of the world after rain. All magic and mayhem in the air.

He'd expected her to be sweet, a little bumbling maybe. He'd thought he'd have to show her how to kiss him properly. Arrogant stud indeed!

She licked and nipped at his lips until he opened his mouth. Her gasp seemed to burrow into his very cells. And then there she was, dueling her tongue with his, running away, and then catching him back again. Teasing him by licking at the tip of his tongue. Taunting him by retreating.

She sucked at his tongue and a jolt of current burst through his nerve endings. Soft and warm, her body moved in a tantalizing rhythm that goaded his.

Vikram released his hands from behind him and went for her with a mindless need he didn't understand. He ran his hands, fingers wide, all over the dips and valleys of her body, greedy to touch all of her. Desperate to not miss an inch. Her arms were around his neck, her weight settled onto his legs.

Damn, the woman really knew how to kiss. There was no tentativeness, no holding back. She let herself fly free with a voraciousness that fueled his own.

"How's that?" she asked him innocently, while she paused, her teeth nipping at his neck, sending a bolt of pleasure down his spine.

"You kiss like a woman who knows what she wants," he managed somehow, while her tongue licked at the tiny bruise she'd just given him.

"I like kissing. I used to do it for hours and it drove—"

He sank his fingers into her hair and tugged gently, and she got the hint. "You're right. No ghosts of the past allowed here."

"Talk to me," he whispered, drowning in the luscious scent of her. Usually, he wasn't into chatting during sex. But this encounter with this woman was the farthest thing from his usual anything. He didn't even know what it was. "Tell me what you love about kissing so much."

"I love the anticipation of what comes next. I like how you can do it slow and soft or fast and hard and how your entire body starts thrumming like this…" she punctuated each word with a long kiss with slow flicks of her tongue and Vikram felt as if she'd been sent to steal his sanity. He wanted to tell her they could do a lot of other things like that too fast or slow, soft or hard. That he would be more than happy to help her discover all of them. That he wanted her name and her address and that he wanted her in his bed tomorrow night too.

Instead, he kept quiet and let her drive him mad.

She dragged her mouth to his jaw, then to his neck again.

His fingers tightened on her hips when she caught the skin at his shoulder between her teeth and sucked. A groan ripped through him, his erection pressing painfully against his trousers.

And then she was back to claim his mouth again. This time, it was a soft melding of mouths, an exploration after the initial frenzy. She cupped his cheek and tugged until he looked up.

Her eyes looked like molten pools of desire, her breasts rose and fell in concert with his own breaths. Her mouth was swollen from kissing him, and Vikram wanted more.

"This is good, isn't it? Between us?" she asked.

Vikram dipped his finger into her mouth. His body hummed for the same caress somewhere else when she licked his finger and wrapped her tongue around it. "It's better than good, Dream Girl. It's... fantastic. The number of dirty things I could do to you while you chat away in my ear... I can't wait to discover all of them."

Naina ducked her face into his neck and took a deep breath.

He smelled like leather and whiskey and something else, far too decadent to be anything other than pure Vikram. His heart thundered against hers, his body a lean fortress of warmth and hardness combined. He wasn't rippling with overdeveloped muscles as every other Bollywood hero seemed to be these days, but rather there was a lean, wiry strength to him that surrounded her. She ran her hands over those taut muscles now, loving the solid feel of him.

His mouth, God, she couldn't believe how good it felt against hers. Couldn't believe how he'd let her take the lead. Play with him. Tease and taunt him. And not once had he pushed for more. Not once had he prodded her along as if the kiss was nothing but a precursor to something else. As if it was a necessary punishment he was sitting through just to get to the end result.

No, she wasn't going to compare him to anyone else in her life.

Vikram Raawal, she was realizing, was more of a hero than the world realized. And he was here with her, fully, in this moment. Hers to do whatever she wanted with. But only for tonight. Only now.

There was no future, no happily-ever-after. Not with Vikram Raawal. Not for her. And she wanted more. She wanted everything tonight.

She sent her fingers on a query up his neck, into his thick hair. "Vikram?"

His head jerked up, his light brown eyes intent on her face. His nostrils flared, something almost like victory dancing in his eyes before he turned his gaze back to her fingers. As if he couldn't allow himself to be distracted for too long from her body and its secrets. He kissed, licked and tongued each knuckle with an erotic thoroughness that sent tremors through her lower belly. "Yes, Dream Girl?"

"All those things you mentioned you wanted to do to me, with me…" She licked her suddenly dry lips when he looked up. "Can we do them? Like, right now?"

He straightened up from his lounging position with a grace Naina knew she'd never have. When he'd walked in earlier, he'd looked so polished, sophisticated, so out of her reach he might as well be the sun to her earth. Now, she could see that his lower lip had a small bump where she'd bitten it, his collar had a stain of her lipstick on it and his expensively cut hair stood up in all directions after she'd pulled her fingers through it.

He looked...suitably rumpled. A little changed. More approachable. As if she'd left her mark on him.

Tomorrow, even a few hours later, all those changes would be gone. He would go back to being Vikram Raawal, the man who had a multi-crore industry at his feet, worshipping him, wanting a piece of him. But Naina wanted him to remember tonight—and her—for a long time to come.

He licked her lower lip, before tugging it gently between his teeth. "Are you sure?" he whispered against her mouth.

"Yes, please. One hundred percent," she said fervently.

"How old are you, Dream Girl?"

"Old enough to know my own mind."

"Answer me."

"Twenty-four."

He blew out a breath and shook his head.

"Oh, come on, Vikram, I know you're a few years older than me, but don't go all honorable on me now. I'm all keyed up. If you leave me hanging tonight, I might have to go knock on my ex's door and beg him—"

He pressed his palm to her mouth and Naina licked it. She tasted salt and sweat, and she felt as if she was drunk on a heady cocktail that was all him.

"No, you won't. That rat doesn't deserve you. And I—"

"Do you want the whole lecture about arbitrary constructs again? Because the first one was just a warm-up."

"God, no!"

"This is an experience I want to have with you, not a gift I'm bestowing on you. Not a thing that will devalue me if I give it away. If you think my ex should have respected my no, then you should respect my yes."

"I don't have condoms on me, but I swear to you I'm clean."

She blushed. "I'm clean and on the pill. Have been for a while."

"In preparation for the rat?" he asked, scrunching his face distastefully.

She shrugged. "He dumped me just as I was ready to make that commitment. Finally. Poor guy put in two years' worth of hard work and persuasion and never got to reap the results."

"He's a fool, Dream Girl. And don't talk about yourself like that." He took her mouth in a rough kiss so full of passion that it clearly told her how much control he'd exerted when she'd been all over him earlier. How much he'd let her explore him. His forehead pressed against hers in a gesture that spoke of a tenderness she wouldn't have associated with this man. "So you've never done this before?"

"I hated being constantly pressured. But I knew my mind when I didn't want it. Just as I know for certain that I do now. I want to have sex. With you. Right now, Vikram, if you please?"

"It pleases me a lot. And if you want to stop, anytime, all you have to do is say so."

She nodded, and bit her lip. Excitement fizzed through her like the bubbles in a bottle of the best champagne. She was nervous too, of course.

He was used to women who were size zero and highly sophisticated. She was...nowhere close to either. The dark couldn't hide her little ice-cream bulge, could it? And for all the kissing she'd practiced, she hadn't ever been anywhere near a man's... thing.

His long fingers wrapped around her nape, drawing her down toward him. Another hard, purely possessive kiss that made her breath ragged in her throat. The kiss held promise and demand in equal measures.

She traced her fingers over his collarbone, mesmerized by the play of light on his skin. "Hey, Vikram?"

"Hmm..." he said, licking her lip. "God, I can't get enough of you saying my name."

"Will you tell me how to make it good for you?"

His hand, that had been pulling the hem of her dress up, up and away, stilled. On her highly sensitive knee. His other hand, playing over the overtly bare neckline that her dress exposed, like she was the strings of a guitar, also halted its movements. "What?" His voice sounded so husky that she barely heard him.

"I want this to be really good for you. And except for some bad porn, I don't know my way around a man's…bits. So some instruction would be much appreciated."

"Yeah?"

"Don't you dare laugh at me. This is important to me."

"Move further up on my thighs then. All the way into my lap."

Naina felt fire run down her spine at the command in his voice. There was something to be said for being ordered by the Bollywood heartthrob Vikram Raawal, to climb atop him, like he was her favorite two-wheeler.

"What are you laughing about?"

She let him see the pleasure she was getting out of every minute of this. "Just that, it is kind of fun being ordered around by you."

His nostrils flared, he threw his head back and let out a groan. "I was wrong in my estimation of you."

Keeping her fingers on the solid breadth of his shoulders, Naina did as she was told. He jerked her close the last inch. Her thighs now grazed the muscular sides of his abdomen and beneath her…he was clearly rock hard. And growing.

Head thrown back, Naina let out a soft moan, her hips wriggling until he was at the exact place where she needed him. At the aching place between her thighs. Hands on his shoulders, she rocked back and forth until their combined moans filled the air.

"You feel that, Dream Girl?" he groaned.

"In every cell of my being," Naina replied, a glorious feeling of warmth and desire running through her veins.

"This is already good for me, love. If it gets any better, it will be over too soon."

"Who... What?" Naina managed to say, when every cell in her being was focused on his questing fingertips. Both of his hands were busy under her dress. He had found the supersensitive skin of her inner thighs and was tracing mesmerizing circles without moving any further north. "You should know, my IQ has already been reduced to half."

Again, another quick swipe of his fingers, and Naina gasped when this time the tip of an index finger grazed the seam of her panties. And then, he was there. Or rather, his wickedly clever fingers were. Playing peekaboo with the seam of her panties. When one finger snuck in under the elastic, Naina went rigid. Anticipation was a concentric yearning in her lower belly. When his fingers teased through the curls at her sex, she buried her face in his neck. "I... I didn't shave down there." She thought she might die if he mocked her.

"I told you before, Dream Girl. I want you exactly as you are. As whoever you are." And then he flicked her most sensitive place in a move that sent shivers through every inch of her. His fingers, she realized, were not just clever. He was a maestro expertly playing his instrument of choice. His thumb stayed loyally at that aching center of her entire being, while his other fingers busied themselves, dipping into the wetness she could feel there. "Oh…" She kept saying the same word, all other faculties reduced to only feeling. She went up on her knees to facilitate his fingers exactly where she wanted them. His mouth, pressed against her neck, erupted into a smile and the vibrations of that laughter rocked through Naina, just as arousing as the fingers he was thrusting into her wet heat.

"Look at me, pretty girl," he said then, and Naina flicked her eyes open, despite the fact that all she wanted to do was drown in the sensation he was creating in her sex. All she wanted to do was focus on it, chase it to its end, until she was nothing else but pleasure.

But there was something to looking into the eyes of the man who was more committed to ensuring your pleasure than you had ever been yourself. There was something to locking eyes with a man who wanted you just as much as you wanted him. Vikram's eyes told her silently, said so many things that his mouth didn't. And Naina was okay with that.

"Keep looking at me, and move. Trust your instincts. Tell me what you want me to do. Tell me how fast, or how slow, or how deep. Tell me where you want my fingers. Tell me where you want my mouth. I'm entirely at your disposal, pretty girl."

His words, in concert with his fingers, pulled at the ever-tightening knot in her lower belly. Naina sent her own hands up her belly to her breasts, already achy and desperate for attention, and she tugged down the bodice of the dress. "Here," she whispered. "I need those clever fingers here too."

"My fingers are far too busy right now." His deep voice had an edge to it. A dark, slumbering quality. "Will my mouth do?"

"Yes, please."

He gave her what she asked for. And even more than that.

In the blink of an eye, Naina found herself drowning in sensation that Vikram created. His mouth painted erotic images over her tight nipples. The sound of him licking them was one she'd never forget. He alternated between them as if he was determined to evoke, to conjure, to pull every inch of sensation out of her body that it was capable of feeling.

His mouth, his fingers, his entire body worked in tandem to push her up and up and up. Her spine arched. And then she was there, thrown into a kaleidoscope of colors and sounds and sensations. Her sex contracted and released and still he kept up the relentless rhythm, dragging it out, prolonging the acute pleasure until tears filled her eyes.

She flopped forward onto him, her arms going tight around him, her face dripping with tears and sweat. She didn't care that she was clinging to him. In this moment, he was hers. She needed an anchor, to come down from the cliff she had just jumped off.

But of course, in her moment of vulnerability, she had misjudged him again.

He held her just as tight as she did him, whispering sweet nothings at her temple, telling her how sexy and how thrilling it was to watch her climax. And she knew he was telling her the truth. Because it was there in his voice. Need rippled through him—his words, his tight body, even in the tension across his face. Naina pulled back. It wasn't enough that she had found satisfaction unlike she had ever known before. She wanted him to find it too. She wanted him to remember her forever. She reached for the seam of his trousers and slowly undid the button and the zipper. She refused to look away from him and he held her gaze too, as if he intended to see into her soul. "I need your words, pretty girl. I need to know you still want this. I need to know you're as desperate as I am in this moment."

"I want you inside me, Vikram. I want you to find satisfaction in my body just as I found it in yours. I want you to wake up tomorrow and think *Oh, my God, that girl rocked my world.*" She dropped her nose against his and smiled up at him. "Is that clear enough?"

"It might hurt. For just a little while."

"I trust you will make it all better after the hurt," she said, a taunt in her tone.

"Of course I will, Dream Girl. Kiss me again," he said simply and Naina complied.

Their kisses went from soft to intense in a matter of seconds. She went from loose and sated to greedy and aroused in minutes. With his hands and mouth, Vikram was everywhere on her skin. Kissing, nipping, licking, until she was a single mass of thrumming sensation. Slowly, he built her up again, until she was panting. Until she was so close to the edge that she could taste it.

He lifted her up and over him, and in the next blink, he was inside her, in a single thrust.

Naina gasped at the thread of pain.

"Shh…look at me, love. Stay here with me," he said, and Naina let his words wash through her. Over her. In this way, he felt as if he was everywhere inside her.

He didn't move. Or even wiggle his hips.

Eyes closed, Naina ran her hands over him. Over that sharp blade of a nose, the surprisingly sweet-tasting mouth, the line of his jaw, to the thud of his heart, to the tautly fascinating map of his abs…her fingers boldly moved down further, to where they were joined together.

Digging her fingers into his shoulders, she pushed up with her thighs and rose up a little, then sank back down. The friction was amazing, the pinch of pain already fading. She did it again, gasping at the thrill that shot through her spine, the tightening knot there…

He moved his palms all over her, just as she'd done to him. Those clever fingers molding and squeezing… "How do you feel now, Dream Girl?"

"It's like a sweet ache, a sense of overwhelming fullness. Vikram?"

His tongue licked at the rigid knot of her nipple. Then he closed those lips over it and tugged, repeating the action, again and again. "Yes, baby?"

"I want to come again," she declared, without an ounce of shyness this time.

She felt his smile near her heart, felt his fingers abandon her breast and when she protested, he took her mouth in such a rough kiss that she felt burned. And then she felt him there, rubbing at her bud, whispering into her ear. "I wish I was a man of beautiful words, Dream Girl." With every word, he thrust up, while pushing his finger down at her center, creating sensations that were amplified a thousand times. "I wish I could describe to you in this moment how beautiful you are…the flush on your skin, the tremble of your lips, the pulse at your neck.

"But I can give you what you want. Tell me again, Dream Girl."

"I want everything. Tonight. Everything you can give me."

And before she could blink, he was lifting her up again, this time pressing her back onto the lounger. And then he was moving inside her again, more deeply than before.

A slow, hard thrust that would have thrown her off the lounger if he wasn't holding her. A swivel of his hips, then another slow drag and every time he did it, the slab of his muscles rubbed her in just the right place and Naina thought she might die if she didn't climax soon.

As if he heard her unsaid plea, his movements became faster, harder, his fingers digging into her hips, causing delicious points of pain that made all the other sensations she was feeling even sharper and brighter.

When Naina would have screamed in ecstasy at the top of her lungs, he covered her mouth with his and swallowed up her pleasure. "Look at me, Dream Girl," he whispered and Naina did and saw his own explosion of pleasure transform his face into a thing of beauty that she would never forget.

This night, this man, these moments of pure, joyous pleasure… Naina knew she was forever changed by it.

CHAPTER FOUR

"VIKRAM RAAWAL'S LATEST blockbuster is nothing more than a cheesy, gratuitously violent, sexist romp…"

"Hell, Rita, turn the bloody radio off!"

Without waiting for a reply, Vikram hung up the phone and then slammed his hand against the steering wheel.

God, he'd just snapped at his very pregnant secretary for no fault of hers. But listening to the same lousy headlines that had been on every TV and radio station for the last week meant his temper was hanging by a thin thread.

Pulling his Range Rover onto the unpaved land at the back of his grandmother's bungalow, he called Rita back, and begged for forgiveness. He laid his head back against the seat and exhaled. Of course, the media was having a field day with the criticism being showered on his latest hit, even though it was raking it up at the box office.

But for once Vikram didn't really give a damn about the bad publicity even, if the entire world thought he was a sellout. If the whole lot of them boycotted his movies.

He *should* care, however.

This was business and he'd always looked at it without getting bogged down by sentiment or ego or prejudice.

But he couldn't give a damn, if he tried. *That* was more worrying than any of the cutting reviews.

"Your life is going to turn upside down."

The grave announcement the astrologer his sister Anya visited every month had made after looking at Vikram's star chart came back to him now. He'd only gone because Anya had insisted. And because Anya had been rather quiet recently and that had worried him.

Worrying about his crazy family's antics was second nature to him ever since he'd found out as a young man that in just a few short years his father had gambled away the entire fortune his grandfather had amassed and that Raawal House was on the verge of collapse. Then came the worry about Virat's daredevil ways after the huge fallout between him and his parents. Then it had been Daadi's heart attack. Then discovering his eighteen-year-old sister was pregnant with a fortune hunter's child, who'd hightailed it out of town the minute he'd realized Anya wasn't the easy express train to fame and fortune.

He *didn't like* involving himself in their lives, as Virat had claimed during their recent fight. He was not a *"pain in the backside control freak who got his kicks from directing his family members' lives as if they were his expensive ivory chess pieces."*

Virat had always had a way with words. But Vikram refused to feel guilty.

Their own parents' incapability of actually acting like parents had forced him into that surrogate role. For as long as he could remember, he'd protected Virat and Anya. Was he supposed to suddenly stop doing it now? Of course, he'd been angry and defensive when he'd asked Virat to prove with his actions that he could be responsible for himself. Which had spiraled into yet another row over what was the definition of respectability and responsibility.

You've forgotten what it is to take risks, Vikram. You've forgotten what it means to live.

Having spent his entire childhood with parents who thrived on drama and chaos, Vikram loathed losing control. He hated the chaos that emotional vulnerability brought with it. He hated being dependent on anyone else for his happiness. God, he'd lived his life like that all through his childhood and adolescence.

He'd worked hard to bring order to the chaos, and yet suddenly, he felt like he was losing it all now. In both his professional and personal lives. His agent had recently informed him that the music director Vikram had wanted for his production company's next film had refused to be involved in the project. The man was brilliant and had always hated Vikram's guts.

The only silver lining from the entirety of this

year had been the few hours he'd spent with Dream Girl at the party last week. He rubbed a hand over his face and laughed. God, he was actually referring to her as Dream Girl in his own head now. Surely he was going insane.

It had been a one-night stand. He'd had one-night stands before. God, yes, the sex, the connection between them had been extraordinary.

But the woman and the memory of the few hours he'd spent with her wouldn't leave him alone. He wanted her. Again. But she clearly didn't want him. Not for anything more than a few hours of fantasy. Because she hadn't got in touch with him. And he still didn't know who she was. He'd fallen asleep for just a couple of minutes in the quiet darkness of the library and when he'd jerked awake, she'd vanished into thin air.

However, what had become inconveniently clear to him over the last week was how much he wanted to believe her when she'd assured him she'd keep their tryst a secret. And his cynical assumption that she'd reveal herself to him, to the whole world, sooner or later.

After all, he was Vikram Raawal. Every woman wanted a piece of him.

God, he could just see those twinkling eyes widen and her mouth narrow in disapproval before she told him he shouldn't believe his own egotistical hype so much.

A strange cocktail of relief and disappointment

coursed through him. Relief because their strange encounter couldn't be unmarred by reality now.

He'd seen enough of life to know the kind of visceral connection they'd shared couldn't be sustained. A few more hours together and she would have surely disappointed him. And he'd have disillusioned her with his own cynical nature.

He should be thankful she hadn't reappeared.

He was thirty-six and clearly in the middle of a midlife crisis. On a good day, he was cynical, grumpy and an unsentimental bastard who only cared about his family's reputation and creating the next hit for Raawal House. He didn't know what a healthy relationship between a man and woman even constituted. For all his stardom, and wealth and "stunning good looks," he wasn't any woman's best chance at a long, happy relationship.

Dream Girl…wasn't just any woman, though. God, she was only twenty-four, a veritable novice when it came to life experience. And yet, she'd been so mature. So funny. So…full of life. So damn sexy. So…out of his reach, for all the power and privilege he held in his palm.

And for the first time in his life, he really wanted something very badly and yet couldn't have it.

His mood went from grumpy to downright crabby when he entered his grandmother's bungalow and discovered Virat had stolen away Daadi for the day. He accepted Ramu Kaka's offer of a cup of chai instead of immediately heading out.

Daadi's yearly pilgrimage to London meant she'd leave tomorrow. Since he had to be on a flight to the Maldives in a few days, he wouldn't see her again for three months.

Three months was a long time when one's grandmother was eighty-three years old. A flash of fear struck him straight in his chest at the thought of the world without Daadi in it. It was infuriating to realize some things would always be out of one's control. Especially the things that mattered the most.

Like Daadi, and Dream Girl.

He laughed so hard that tears pricked his eyes. Daadi and the Dream Girl sounded like the title of one of those artsy, cutting comedy films that a brilliant genius like Virat would make. His cell phone rang.

He yelled at Virat, got scolded by Daadi for yelling, and then made her promise she'd be back in two months this time rather than three.

"Vicky, *beta*, look after Naina for me, *haa*?" Daadi said, finally getting to the point. "She's trying to find work in the film industry and it's not like you to be harsh toward someone so innocent."

He hung up, after promising Daadi he would look after that "poor innocent lamb" with the decidedly cutting tongue. But like it or not, he did owe the woman an apology, for more than one thing. Grumpy and arrogant he might be, but he knew when to admit he was wrong. And he had been kind of nasty to her.

The creaky whine of the old gramophone player and an old, slow song cut into his quiet reverie. He thought the language might be Tamil, but he didn't understand the words. The soulful melody suited his own mood perfectly. He took the winding stairs up, toward the sound coming from one of the back bedrooms, anticipation building inside him, just as the melody came to a crescendo.

He found Naina Menon crooning softly along with the song, her small nose noticeably red, wrapping a beautiful, expensive-looking green sari in layers of tissue paper with the utmost care. A battered-looking suitcase lay open behind her, with a rumpled duffel bag. The bracelets she wore on one wrist tinkled every time she spread out another layer of tissue paper.

The song went through a particularly maudlin stretch. Ms. Menon laid her head against the wall, bringing one knee up. Losing herself completely in the song. She wasn't crying and yet Vikram felt as if she was on the verge of it. He couldn't move, transfixed by the simple and yet stunning beauty of the woman.

He'd always considered the expression of too much emotion to be a vulgar display. Maybe because he'd been exposed to such excessive amounts of it while growing up. Every day, there had been some unavoidable drama with his parents, until Daadi, who'd been living with them since his grandfather died, had moved out again, bringing Vikram with her back to this bungalow.

But Ms. Menon…it was obvious she was struggling with something. Her entire body seemed to move as one with the song.

She wore another oversized yellow kurta over blue jeans, with those dangling earrings again, and her untamed hair was held together by a small clip that was clearly losing its fight. Jet-black corkscrew curls framed a halo around her face. A colorful, flimsy scarf hung around her neck, a long, beaded necklace with a metallic pendant moving every time she took a deep breath.

She looked like the words from the song given beautiful form. Words he didn't understand technically and yet the meaning they conveyed sank deep into his bones.

Loneliness. A desperate need for comfort. The very human need for companionship.

The song thrummed through him with a familiarity he didn't understand. He looked anew at the woman, marveling at how easily he could sense her own confusion, pain and something else.

His first impression of her had been of a deceptively plain woman. And the flash of attraction he'd felt for her had blindsided him. She wasn't his type.

Although, after the encounter with Dream Girl, he was rethinking arbitrary constructs like types. Questioning everything he'd been conditioned to think from a young age thanks to his constant exposure to the film industry. About beauty and art and authenticity. About the masks they all wore.

Now, in this moment, he realized calling Naina Menon plain was like calling a sunflower boring compared to some exotic, temperamental flower. Slowly, the song came to an end. The deep breath she took sent her breasts rising and falling and he watched, far too fascinated.

A breeze flew through the open windows, and the scarf flew away from her neck, revealing a fading pinkish-blue smudge on the area between her neck and shoulder.

Vikram stiffened, a thread of something piercing him with a sudden intensity.

She looked up and jerked. "How did you find…"

Coming away from the wall, she slammed her palm against her mouth and launched onto her feet so fast that she stumbled over the open suitcase lying at her feet.

It sent her toppling forward.

Vikram reached for her instantly, trying to overcome her momentum. She fell onto him with a thud that knocked her head into the underside of his chin. His teeth rattled inside his mouth and a wave of pain vibrated up his jaw. But even through the jarring sensation, there was a familiarity in the way her body pressed against his. A subtle wisp of a jasmine scent teasing his nostrils. A fragment of sound that had fallen from her mouth that reminded him of how Dream Girl had sounded when she…

"Let me go." He heard the words as if through a long tunnel, while scents and sensations poured through him. "Please. I'm fine," she said, louder this time, and Vikram released his hold.

She rubbed at her wrist as though his touch had

burned her. "I'm sorry," he said, not surprised to find his voice gruff.

Did this midlife crisis mean he was going to behave like a randy goat with every woman he came across? Hadn't Virat teased him he was turning grumpier than usual because *"your testosterone levels are falling and you clearly aren't the powerful, macho guy who attracts all the women anymore"*?

With Naina Menon's warm imprint still on his own body, Vikram felt no lack of testosterone flowing through him. In fact, it felt like his libido was working overtime for the short contact had made his every nerve ending sing with desire.

"No, don't apologize." Ms. Menon cleared her throat, and when she spoke again, she sounded different, in control. "Thanks for catching me. You saved me from a bad fall."

He didn't say anything. Just stared at her, a hint of premonition gathering at the base of his neck, tightening it unbearably.

This uptight, self-righteous, morality inspector couldn't be his fun, bold, sexy Dream Girl, could she?

"What were you about to say when you saw me?" he demanded, the words coming out of his mouth in a rush.

A slight dusting of pink claimed her cheeks and she turned away. "Nothing. My thoughts were somewhere else." She threw a look at him over her shoulder. As if to confirm he was still there. "Daadiji left with Virat and your sister. Anya kept saying you wanted to see your grandmother, but he didn't listen. They won't be back tonight and Daadiji is leaving for London tomorrow."

When he didn't show any sign of leaving, she turned around again, folding her arms under her breasts. "Is there anything else I can help you with?"

"Are you dismissing me from my own home, Ms. Menon?" he said, suddenly feeling a lot more comfortable. Riling her up, he was realizing, was making his own grumpy mood better.

She opened her mouth, closed it, then opened it again.

"You're upset. What's happened?" he asked softly. Something was off about her reaction to him. About his reaction to her. About this whole thing.

"I'm not upset," she denied, her voice full of a shakiness that belied her words. Her dark brown gaze met his briefly and again, he felt that jolt of electricity thrum through him. Another pair of beautiful eyes the exact same dark brown as hers had held his gaze boldly while he'd lost himself in her warmth.

He walked across the room, and leaned against the wall. He wanted to sit down but he saw the panic in her eyes, the tensing of her shoulders with every breath he took. She was nervous in his presence.

Because they had argued with each other last time he'd been here? Because she didn't like him? Or for another, much more sensational reason?

She sighed. "I got some news today that upset me a little… On top of learning that Daadiji's leaving for London tomorrow. It's been a too much kind of day."

He nodded absently.

She was the right height for Dream Girl, though that's all he had in the physical arena to go by. There was no way he could have missed that mass of curly hair. But hair could be straightened and he knew first-hand the miracles makeup could achieve.

Not that this woman needed makeup to look stunning.

So if it was her, why all the secrecy? What did she hope to achieve by pretending as if they didn't know each other in the most intimate way? Had it truly been a fantasy of a few hours? Damn the woman, why did she have to complicate this by not admitting it?

"I have her permission to stay here tonight. You can call Virat and confirm that if you would like."

"You think I'm waiting to throw you out right now?"

She shrugged.

Vikram bit his lip and then went for it. "I apologize for speaking harshly to you the first time we met. And for assigning cheap, utterly unfair motives to your presence here. I have had enough calls from Daadi to understand that she really appreciated your company and assistance these past two months."

"It was my pleasure," she added, without really acknowledging his apology.

So, the woman held grudges, huh? "What were you doing for Virat before you came here to help Daadi?"

"Just some research for another one of his projects. I have a half-finished PhD in film history so I was qualified."

He swallowed his frustration and nodded at the gramophone player.

"What was the song you were listening to?"

"Oh, it's from the nineteen-fifties. I found the record while sorting out your grandfather's old things." For the flash of a second, excitement lit up her face. And he saw that same incandescent quality that had held him breathless in the dim light of the library. "Some of those records are priceless. Your grandmother said I could have this one. But if you want it—"

"I don't give a rat's ass about that old record. Stop casting me as some mustache-twirling villain."

Her mouth twitched, but she still didn't meet his gaze.

"Tell me what the song means," he said, wanting to see that joy return to her eyes.

She frowned. "Why?"

"There's no ulterior motive, Ms. Menon. I know most songs from that era but I'd never heard of that one."

"It's in Tamil," she said.

"I do know songs outside of Hindi. Raawal House used to produce a lot of South Indian movies at that time."

"It's by this lady who didn't find a lot of commercial success. In fact, I think it's the only film that she sang for."

"How do you know so much about it?"

"Oh, it was my mother's favorite song. I heard it all the time growing up. She would play it and walk around our house acting out the song. She was very… Do you understand the words?"

He shook his head.

"She's saying goodbye to someone she loves. Mama always said the best thing we could do for ourselves was to understand what we were feeling. It's hard to acknowledge our own emotions sometimes. Especially when they make us realize something uncomfortable about ourselves. It's strange, isn't it?"

The restlessness within him this last year, this constant need for something more in his life and yet not knowing what the more was…her words suddenly made him understand himself a little better.

She wasn't aware of him anymore, caught up in whatever put that look in her eyes. "What's strange?" he asked quietly.

"Even until last year, that song was a big source of comfort to me. I'd play it and go back to those happy times where I trailed behind her through the house. Now, it feels like the song doesn't have that same sense of comfort and familiarity that I associated with it for so long.

"I feel like I've lost her all over again."

"Maybe it's just your perception of yourself that's changing, Ms. Menon. Maybe you simply aren't that heartbroken little girl anymore. Maybe you're coming into your own and no longer need the false comfort of an old song," he said, holding her gaze.

Falling into those beautiful brown depths one

word at a time. There was honesty and intelligence
and such strength in those eyes. Such heart and heat
in them. Just like that, suddenly he knew. In his
heart, of all places, which he could truthfully say had
never before known anything with such certainty.

Naina Menon was his Dream Girl.

"Are you mocking me?"

He blinked. "Not at all."

Thoughts and consequences ran through his head
like a film on fast forward. What did it mean? Why
had she done it? Was he simply supposed to behave
as if that night hadn't happened? Was that what she
meant to do? The idea of leaving it up in the air, the
idea of just…letting that night remain between them
like some fantasy illusion made the hair on his neck
stand up. "In fact, this is probably the second most
meaningful conversation I've had in years."

Her head jerked up, her eyes searching his face
with an intensity that bordered on interest. No, something more. Not fear, no. She wasn't afraid of him.
The last thing he wanted was for Naina to think he'd
abuse his power in this, his knowledge of her identity in any way. "Then that sounds incredibly wise."

"I'm not all perfect good looks," he said wickedly,
wondering if by repeating what she'd said to him
that night, he could draw out a confession from her.

"Wow, looks, a sense of humor and a deep understanding of my psyche. I almost want to put your
poster up on my wall again."

"Did you have my poster up on your wall, Ms.
Menon?" he asked smoothly.

She blinked and it was all Vikram could do to stop himself from reaching for her.

He tucked his hands behind him to arrest the overwhelming impulse. Damn it, the woman had been playful and funny at the ball and he'd lapped it up. Today, she looked bashful and wary and he still liked her. Whatever facet she revealed of herself, he had a feeling he would appreciate it.

"A long time ago, yes. After your first movie. Most of the heroes were older men for decades and then there was suddenly you, the boy next door, the college student, the idealistic young man. No wonder it launched you into stardom.

"I'm not that schoolgirl anymore. And you're not perfect hero material, this larger-than-life boy whose broad shoulders could carry every girl's dreams. You're..."

Their eyes locked and Vikram had the strangest sensation. As if anticipation was his breath, ballooning up in his chest. Waiting for more words from this woman who seemed to see through him with such unsettling ease. Waiting for more of her devastating insight.

"What am I now, Ms. Menon?"

"You're...human," she said simply. "Like the rest of us."

A lightness filled his entire being and Vikram felt as if he had moved from the shadows into bright sunshine. As if, after living in the harsh, unnatural spotlight of fame all his life, he was suddenly being seen for the very first time.

"Which also means you're my equal." He laughed at the relief that poured through him. "Not that it was ever in question."

A hint of pink crept up her cheeks. He felt like he'd won something for the simple fact of surprising her. "Did I render you mute? Then I guess I'm not as bad with words as Virat would like us all to believe."

"I don't think you're bad with words at all, Mr. Raawal. I think you just don't feel people are usually worth using that skill on."

"How did she die? Your mother?"

She turned to him and the ache of grief in her eyes almost knocked him flat. "She didn't. She walked out on my father and me when I was ten. Left a note saying her heart wasn't in the life we had and disappeared in the middle of the night."

He felt a burst of such fury on her behalf that he couldn't speak for a few minutes. "I'm sorry about that." He racked his mind for more words. The right thing to say. "There were days I wished my mother or father had walked out in the middle of the night," he finally said.

She laughed and then sobered up, all before he could blink twice. "Oh, that's such an awful thing to say. Thanks for trying to make me feel better, Mr. Raawal, but you're absolutely horrific at it."

"I really wasn't joking."

"Of course, you..." Her mouth fell open and she closed it with a click. "I'm sorry about...that."

He shrugged, pretending to not show how shocked he was by his own admission. He could see it in her eyes too. He never ever spoke to the media about his family. It was none of their business. His parents had provided enough fodder for the gossips with their high-profile separations every time his father was unfaithful and the subsequent reunions every time his mother forgave him, resulting in an endless vicious cycle of hate and love.

In the beginning, fixing the reputation of Raawal House had been an act of survival. With all the company's assets tied up in sinking films and unwise investments, the only thing he'd had to start with was the respect and prestige his grandfather Vijay Raawal's name still commanded in some circles. Producers and investors had trusted him, his word, had seen something in him that had reminded them of Daadu.

For fifteen years, he'd forced his family by every means available to him, to behave. Constantly herding them to walk a respectful line so that he could rebuild the reputation of Raawal House.

But somewhere along the line, he'd lost his own way. He'd started believing in his own invincibility. He'd started overcompensating for all the negative attention his parents had brought to the family by keeping Virat and Anya on too tight a leash and then condemning them for any missteps they might take. By stifling them. His need to keep them safe and secure, to protect them from the same kind of chaos that had disrupted his childhood and adolescence had been somehow twisted up and morphed into needing to control every minute detail of their lives.

Of his own life.

But with Naina, it was easy to speak of his family. Easy to share the tales of dysfunction and drama that had made up most of his childhood. Though he had absolutely no idea how they'd ended up trading childhood pain of all things. Crossing swords was more their style, wasn't it?

And if this woman was his Dream Girl too…she'd unraveled him not once, but twice now. Every rational instinct in him, every voice he'd honed to be in total control of himself warned him to get the hell out of there. To walk away from her and never return.

Instead, he said, "My mother wasn't the most spectacular actress in Bollywood over the span of two decades for nothing. After a while, I think she saw no distinction between her public persona and the private one. Anyway, I survived. I had Daadi at the worst of times." Thinking of this fierce woman in front of him as a lost, motherless little girl made his chest tight. "I hope you had someone too."

"I had Papa." She scrunched her brow. "Or rather he had me. He was devastated by her leaving. We somehow muddled through. Later, he married my stepmother. She and her daughter Maya…" She smiled, and there was that fleeting happiness in her eyes again. "We became each other's saving grace. Have you heard of my stepmother Jaya Pandit? She's also an actress, although she's not hugely successful."

He nodded, vaguely remembering a short, pretty woman with intelligent eyes and a colorful personality. "She's the one developing a reputation for being difficult and abrasive. Didn't she get into a mad scuffle with some producer and that ridiculous TV channel got it all on camera?"

She winced and Vikram regretted the distaste he was sure had shown on his face. "It's easy for you to look down on her. But that's the only way Jaya Ma knows how to survive in your horrid industry. She put on fifteen kilos for a role only to be told by the producer that he'd given it to his wife's cousin. It's been…hard for her. If she isn't being turned down for being too loud, she's simply forgotten."

"The other news you got to make it a 'too much kind of day'…is it about her?"

"No, my stepsister Maya got accepted to a university in the States. She'll be leaving soon." She tried to hide the pain in her eyes with an empty smile. But one thing was certain; this woman was no actress.

She wore her emotions on her face with such an artless honesty that Vikram found it hard to look at. It was like looking straight at the sun and you couldn't do it for too long. You simply closed your eyes and basked in the warmth of it. "I'll miss her… she's my sister and best friend rolled into one. I'm thrilled for her though." A forced chuckle this time. "She's the brilliant one in the family. And the beauty, too, actually."

"You had no idea that she'd even applied to study abroad, did you? And yet you value her so much."

She shrugged. "Maya's always talked about pursuing a career in academia, getting into one of the prestigious research laboratories. Which segues perfectly into…" She looked up. Shoulders straight, she took a deep breath. Readying for battle? "Daadiji mentioned your secretary is going on maternity leave early because of complications, and that you're looking for an urgent temporary stand-in until her proper replacement arrives. Give me the chance to work for you."

"What?"

"I want to come work for you. You're going on a writing trip to the Maldives for a few weeks, right? With Daadiji going to London for the next two months, I'm available and I'm also kind of cash-strapped."

"You must be desperate if you're willing to work for me, Ms. Menon."

She picked up the notepad that had been sitting on the bed. Vikram saw the numbers she'd been adding up and scratching out, before she hid it behind her back. Even with the quick glimpse he got, it was clear the second column far outweighed the first. "I have a lot of expenses," she said evasively.

"Why can't your sister get a job?"

"I told you. She just got admitted into a renowned university. She can't give up her education."

"What was it you said about your half-finished PhD?"

"I had to quit when Papa became very ill because someone had to nurse him; Maya was too busy and Jaya Ma too distressed to do it. Now, with the medical bills and the loan payment on the house, without Maya earning a paycheck, it will be very tight. I can't afford to go back and finish my PhD."

He reached around her to grab the pad. Embarrassment filled her cheeks. "We've all been there, Ms. Menon. What's the loan for?" he asked, tapping the big number.

"Papa took a loan against the house to pay for Jaya Ma's cosmetic procedures to enable her to get more film roles, but she still hasn't found enough work. If I don't keep up with the payments, the bank will seize the house I grew up in. We rent it out because it's cheaper for us to share a flat."

Ten different ideas rose to his mouth about how she could cut these expenses in half. But he kept them to himself. The last thing he wanted to do was make her defensive again. "You will have no...problems taking orders from me? Haven't you heard the horror stories about how this industry treats personal assistants?"

"None of them have been about you. In fact, you have the stellar reputation of being a fair boss. Even Jaya Ma has nothing bad to say about you and believe me, she has an opinion on everyone."

"Ahh...but none of my staff has ever laid into me with such cutting condemnation about my life."

She nodded. "Of course, I said things to you that I had no right to."

He crossed his legs and smiled. But deep inside, he was sorely disappointed. Was she going to turn out like the rest of the damn world now? Pander to him just because she wanted something from him? Stroke his ego all out of proportion because he was in a position to help her out financially? "I'm all ears if you want to apologize."

"I agree that I had no right to say those words to you. But it doesn't mean that what I said was untrue. Even if I say sorry, it won't really be genuine. So do you still want my apology?"

A thrill shot through him at the defiant tilt of her chin.

There was an undeniable attraction between them. He'd known that before she'd bitten into him that very first time. But the interesting thing was that it was still there, shimmering in the air between them. In the way she greedily studied his face but looked away when he met her gaze.

In the way the air charged between them.

That was two unusual women that had snared his attention in less than one week. Not a coincidence at all—seeing as they were the same person.

But Dream Girl had made it clear that she'd been looking for a fantasy for only one night.

"You're consistent, Ms. Menon. I'll give you that."

"I couldn't stand it if you thought I was a hypocrite."

"For God's sake! Don't be ashamed of wanting a better life. Of using the opportunities and people that come your way to build that better life. Or you'll be left behind while they all use you to climb up their own ladder. Like I assume your stepmother and stepsister are doing."

"That's a horrible thing to say about them! Jaya Ma and Maya are my family."

"And you think family doesn't manipulate and use you?"

"Please, don't. You don't know us. If you want me to say sorry for everything I've ever said to you and beg you for this job, then I will do it. I'm—"

He pressed his hand against her mouth in a sudden move that surprised even him. His heartbeat was loud in his ears as the incredible softness of her mouth pressed into his palm. The warmth of her lips singed his skin. The skin of her jaw was silky under the pads of his fingers and he wanted to keep them there forever.

Eyes wide, she stared at him. The same sensual shock traveled through him. There was something about this woman that undid him on a level he didn't understand. That made excitement thrum through his blood.

"No, Ms. Menon," he finally said, pulling away his hand. No movement had ever cost him as much willpower as he'd just had to exert to pull away from her. "I will not be responsible for bringing you that low. I won't have that sin at my feet."

For once, she said nothing. Only continued to stare at him as if she meant to eat him up.

He moved away from her, wondering if he was going mad. Was he actually considering her request? This woman knew him like no one else did. She wanted to go on pretending that they had not been intimate with each other on a level that moved beyond just the physical. She…had the knack of twisting him up, of shaking up rules he'd lived by for years. And still…

If he took away this opportunity from her when

she clearly needed it, what kind of a man did it make him?

Was he going to hold the insanity of that night against her? Was he going to be a petulant little man, a shadow of his father, just because she wouldn't admit to him that she wanted him?

God, no!

And even if she admitted to him that it had been her, what would he do with that information? Offer her another one-night stand? A fling that would only hurt her in the end? A relationship that he would walk away from as soon as he became bored? Because, it was inevitable that he would.

He turned around to face her. "If I agree, there will be a clear hierarchy between us. I would be your boss and you my assistant. Not my personal morality advisor. Neither will I allow a repetition of those lectures you're really fond of spouting."

"Right, of course! You won't even know I'm there, except to say yes to whatever you say." She took a deep breath. "And after it's over, you'll never hear from me again."

"What the hell does that mean?" he said with a frown, not liking that idea one bit. Just like that, she got under his skin again. Made dust of his own damned rules. "I thought your aim was to work in the film industry. Or did I misunderstand Daadi?"

She shrugged. "It's clear that you're doing this to honor Daadiji's wishes to look after me, Mr. Raawal. I won't take advantage of her good nature or your sense of obligation. I don't like lingering where I'm not wanted."

"No, you prefer to hide from real life, don't you? From your stepmother, from your stepsister, from… anything that's uncomfortable, no? You prefer to escape. Live life in stolen moments under darkness and disguises."

Her hands fisted by her sides, her eyes glinting with a brightness that made them look like large pools. Anger vibrated from her, as honest and pure as the laughter she'd delighted him with that night.

He waited, breath on hold, for her to lose the tightly held control, to come at him, cutting words and all. His heart beat at a pace that drummed loud in his ears. It shook him to realize how much he wanted her to admit it had been her that night at the ball.

How much he wanted to see the same laughter and desire in her eyes when she looked at him now. Whatever common ground they'd achieved unwittingly in the last hour was gone now. And maybe it was for the best, he realized, especially if they were to spend several weeks together in close quarters.

"You don't know anything about me," she said finally, her breasts still rising and falling. "Not my fears, nor my dreams."

With that fierce statement, she firmly slammed the door on the self-indulgent drama he was forcing on them both. Not by a flicker of an eyelid did she show that she got his pointed remark about living life under darkness and disguises. But… Vikram knew that face. He'd witnessed the most intimate pleasure and joy and irreverence written on it even while it had been more than half covered by the mask she'd worn.

And that was for the best. There was no permutation of events in which he could see her in his future on a permanent basis.

"Your days and nights will be mine, Ms. Menon. I will ask you to fetch coffee, dry cleaning, send gifts to friends and family, even break up with my exes. Are you quite sure you have the constitution to quietly take orders from me without any further preaching?"

There was a minute hesitation he'd have missed if he wasn't obsessed with every nuance of her face. "I'll just pretend that you're the most fascinating man I've ever met. And keep any criticism to myself."

"Oh, I wouldn't want you to curb your opinions, Ms. Menon. What would the world be if it didn't have your tart tongue in it?"

He walked out of her room, leaving her steaming mad. His own mouth was curved into a wide smile and Vikram realized he hadn't felt this good in a long time. If ever.

CHAPTER FIVE

"YOU PREFER TO live life in stolen moments under darkness and disguises."

Vikram's parting shot still haunted her as the taxi drove along a narrow, winding road on the outskirts of the city leading to a private airfield.

Had he already realized she was the woman from the masked ball?

No, he couldn't. She looked so different, he couldn't possibly have recognized her.

That comment had to be his way of aggravating her, as he'd done from the beginning. Getting under her skin just because she'd criticized him.

Why would he give her a job if he knew she was Dream Girl? If he had, he'd have thrown her out of his grandmother's house because he'd automatically assume she was cooking up some nefarious scheme to trap him. At best, he'd have openly asked what her game plan was.

The man that the world saw, and who she had seen initially, was a hardened cynic. Except he hadn't been on the night of the party or a few days ago when he'd asked her about the meaning of her mother's favorite song.

When he'd talked about his own family, when he'd asked after hers, he had been genuine. Oh, of course he was still arrogant, coming to the conclusion that her family were taking advantage of her. But beneath that arrogance, there had been understanding too.

Which had prompted her to blurt out this idea of working for him.

For a few weeks, in gorgeous Maldives, all she'd need to do was keep her head down. Figure out where her future lay after what had happened with Rohan and now that Maya was moving on. Think of how best to save the house.

She paid off the taxi driver, wincing over all the crisp notes she pressed into his hand. It was the price of her pride. Of course, her new boss had offered to pick her up on the way to the private airport on the outskirts of Mumbai that she'd had no idea even existed.

But that meant spending more time in Vikram's company while that gaze of his drilled into her. Being coherent while he permeated the space around her with his vital masculinity was too much to ask of herself right now.

Before that night, her old teenage infatuation with him had been silly, one-dimensional, completely based in fantasyland. Fueled by her mooning over him for years.

Yes, he'd been funny and approachable and let's

not forget, hot. But now…now she knew the man and she found him even more fascinating, to say the least.

The taxi driver mumbled something about living the high life and Naina turned away with a smile. He'd no idea how much she wanted to crawl back into the taxi and run away from the man waiting for her on the plane.

That night in the library had been just an accident of nature—like the meteor that hit earth every hundred years. It had shaken up the very foundation of her life and she was still processing the tremors it had left behind. But she knew she couldn't survive a second impact.

With that resolve sorted in her head, she walked up the airplane stairs just as it started to rain, anticipation thrumming through her.

Elegant cream-and-white leather greeted her as she stepped inside, the main cabin more spacious than the entire flat she shared with her stepmom.

Seven pairs of eyes focused on her for a few seconds, took in her pink blouse and colorful skirt and then promptly ignored her. Somehow, she kept her squeal locked away when she recognized her favorite playwright.

From all the information Vikram's secretary had told her over a long phone call, Naina knew she'd be working hard for every rupee she earned over the next few weeks. But talking to Rita without Vikram staring down at her had also helped her realize she could do this job well.

For so long after Mama had left, it had been she

who had tried to wrangle the household accounts into some semblance of order, despite her young age. Papa had been so lost without his wife. It had been all he could do to hold onto his tenure at the university.

When he had married her stepmother, Naina had given up control of the family finances to her. Looking back, she should have realized Jaya Ma had no impulse control, whether it came to emotions or finances. She had felt so betrayed when her father had died and she'd discovered the extent of the debts but had shoved the negative emotion away, because really, what was the point? There had been so many things to take care of after he'd died that indulging in her feelings would have been nothing but a petty waste of time.

She handed her pathetic-looking duffel bag into the all-too-elegant flight attendant's hands. After requesting a cup of coffee, Naina settled down into her luxurious, buttery soft leather seat and looked around the unusual assortment of people onboard.

As well as the playwright, there were the Sharmas, who were a writing team of husband and wife, a septuagenarian cinematographer that she recognized only because her father had made it a point to show Naina the vintage movies the man had made, a well-known female novelist, with a man Naina didn't recognize cozying up to her, and the last, a smartly dressed young man around her age with fashionable spectacles and a sharp nose. And a dazzlingly hot smile.

Grateful for a friendly face, Naina joined him.

It took three minutes for them to discover that Ajay was the son of a friend of a colleague of a cousin of Papa's and that he also believed it a great loss that many fabulous filmmakers from South India were barely known outside of their region.

Ajay was even more nervous than her, because while Virat had recommended him to Vikram, he'd never worked for the big Mr. Raawal before. He'd also gathered from industry gossip that Vikram and Virat butted heads quite a lot, so he wasn't sure how long his employment might last.

Naina did her best to allay his fears, by distracting Ajay with questions about his work. His portfolio—Ajay was an artist and set designer—was magnificent.

Whatever this project was, she was thrilled to see its conception. "Your work speaks for you," she said, after gushing over all the period costume pieces and sets in his sketchbook.

"These are just rough sketches. Virat mentioned this film is going to be a period blockbuster with an all-star cast. It's actually Mr. Raawal's dream project that he's been trying to get off the ground for years." Ajay chuckled. "As if anything's impossible for Mr. Raawal. The entire industry bends its knee to him if he so much as blinks in their direction."

Naina didn't like the censure in his voice. Maybe because it's what she had thought too. At first.

"Everyone wants a piece of me," Vikram had said.

"For what it's worth, I've heard Mr. Raawal is a

demanding but fair man to work for," she said, incapable of staying quiet. "I'd say this is your big chance."

Gratitude filling his eyes, Ajay reached for her hand on the table between them and squeezed it. Naina returned his clasp, feeling much better herself. The flight attendant opened the luggage hatch opposite them and put Ajay's bag next to hers.

"At least our bags have each other," he whispered with a wink.

As if on cue, Vikram stepped inside the plane, right at that precise moment.

His broad shoulders filled the not-so-narrow expanse of the aisle. The white shirt he wore was plastered to his chest from the now torrential downpour outside, and he was dripping water all over the floor. The outline of his hard chest reminded her of how delicious it had felt against her naked breasts. His black trousers molded to his strong thighs. His hair was pushed away from his forehead. He looked like her dreams given form.

Naina urgently wanted to go up to him and press her mouth to the pulse beating at his neck. She wanted to push her hands through his wet hair.

A number of greetings rang out around the cabin, cutting into her reverie. His gaze swept through the cabin, slowly, methodically. Her tummy went into a slow roll, every cell prickling with awareness. She knew who he was looking for.

Those dark brown eyes finally landed on her. Their gazes held, for no more than a few seconds.

His, hot and demanding. A jolt of answering hunger rose in her, her body thrumming with anticipation.

Oh, God, how many times had she made fun of seeing lightning in the sky when the hero and heroine met in one of those cheesier romance movies? And yet, lightning striking the jet because of the energy sparking between them didn't seem quite so far-fetched right now.

And then his gaze moved to her hand in Ajay's, to their heads bent together, to the smile that had frozen on her face.

His disapproval was instant. As if the flight attendant had flipped the air-conditioning switch from warm to chilly in a few seconds. A guilty flush of heat climbed up her cheeks. Her smile slipped, but she refused to pull her hand from Ajay's just because Vikram didn't like it.

With a muffled curse, Ajay jerked away from her and buried his face in his portfolio. Naina wanted to throw something at the man still staring down at her as if he owned her.

It wasn't going unnoticed by the rest of the team either. She much preferred their earlier indifference to this sudden curiosity.

Her pulse returned to a normal pace as Vikram finally strode past her. Three long minutes later, he called out her name. She felt like a disobedient child being called to the headmaster's office.

The front cabin had nothing on the sheer luxury that was the rear one, separated by a sturdy beige door. There was a bed in here with cream sheets, that was bigger than the one she'd shared with Maya when they'd been teenagers. A compact en suite bathroom was in one corner, the door slightly ajar to show her a tiny glimpse of a shower with sleek gold fittings. Her mouth was going to perpetually stay open at this rate.

Vikram sat down on the bed and bent over to undo his shoelaces. The wet shirt did wonders to the musculature of his back and all Naina wanted to do was to trace her finger down the line of his spine. And maybe then follow it up with her tongue. And then maybe sink her teeth into that area where his shoulder met his neck. Like he'd done to her just before he'd climaxed inside her.

She didn't want to lose the slight mark he'd given her so she'd been standing lopsided in her shower ever since that night in the library, trying to not let anything that could make it go away touch her skin there. Her fingers went to the spot now.

The wet gurgle of his shoes as he yanked them off made her pull her hand away.

He had caught her watching him. The knowledge was there in his eyes.

"I'm sorry, what?" she said extra politely, realizing he'd said something.

"I asked you if you've—"

"I've gone through the entire to-do list with Rita and run every errand you requested."

He pulled his shirt out from his trousers, pulled it over his head and threw it into a small basket.

"Where's my luggage, Ms. Menon?"

"What?" Naina muttered, now faced with the amazing prospect that was his naked chest. As she'd thought that night at the masked ball, he didn't have one of those stupidly ripped bodies that reminded her of weightlifters pumped up on steroids. What he did have was hard, beautifully defined pectoral muscles, with a sparse coating of hair that converged into a line running down his abs.

Tight, equally well-defined abdominal muscles. That she hadn't touched or licked or kissed yet.

So much wasted opportunity.

"Ms. Menon?"

"What?" she snapped at him.

Towel in hand, he stilled. A wicked glint appeared in his eyes. "You're muttering about wasted opportunities. Do you want to clarify?"

"No," she whispered, face aflame.

"It's clear you're not used to seeing half-naked men. But I was shivering in that thing, which is not very manly of me and I'd hoped you'd bring my stuff in here."

"First of all, I *too* am used to seeing half-naked men," she retorted. *"All the time."*

He waited with a raised brow and a twitching mouth. She sounded like her friend Pinky who'd boasted to have French-kissed a boy when they'd been twelve. Pinky, it turned out, had been licking away at her favorite teddy bear's mouth.

"Secondly, it's entirely manly to shiver when you're in wet clothes. And thirdly, what stuff?"

"My luggage. You were supposed to pick it up."

Mortification painted her face with heat. "Of course, that's why you called me in here. I…" She opened the door, went back to the front cabin, found where the attendant had put it and dragged it back to him. She'd acted like a complete bumbling idiot. And she liked herself the least when she did that.

"Look, you're…" She moved her hand to signal his body. "I just lost my head there for a second. It won't happen again. I'm sorry."

"Are you going to apologize every time I catch you staring at me?"

Affront filled her, like air pumped into a balloon. "I will not… I…" Her shoulders slumped. "I don't stare at every good-looking man, okay? It's just that you…"

"What about me, Ms. Menon?"

The interest in his voice caught her before she admitted what she absolutely couldn't. "I told you, I had a silly little crush on you as a teenager. It catches me out sometimes. That's all."

"That's all, yeah," he said, nodding. He sounded disappointed. "Can you step out for a moment and let me change out of these wet clothes?"

"Sure." She stood outside the door, called herself a hundred names and then walked back in. When she was absolutely certain that he was done showing off his glorious body.

He was stretched out on the bed, a sheaf of papers all around him. A pair of glasses with bifocal lenses rested on his nose. He was wearing a worn-out T-shirt with a comic print on it and sweatpants.

And his big feet were bare. He had nice, long toes and square nails.

Even the man's feet were cute and sexy.

He looked up. "Sit down please."

She sat at the edge of the bed on the opposite side from him. As far away as possible, with one butt cheek hanging off. The whir of the plane's engines filled the background and she scooted up so she didn't fall off.

"I'll allow you a certain amount of leeway for today since this was all very sudden." It was as if he'd amassed patience from the entire world and filled his words with it. "Remember that you're here as my assistant. To be at my beck and call. Not for a vacation or to stir up gossip and definitely not to socialize."

"I was only being friendly," she said hotly, knowing that his lecture had more to do with her chatting to Ajay than any of his other points. "Any gossip in there, you started it. You're the one that looked at me as if you…"

Those beautiful brown eyes trapped hers. "As if I what, Ms. Menon?"

"As if I was the most interesting thing you've ever seen. Now you've got them all riled up with unnecessary curiosity."

"Ahh…yes, that was my fault. You reminded me of someone for a moment." His gaze swept over her—from her hair in a professional-looking bun on top of her head to her knees folded primly and tucked against the bed. Heat licked through her even though it wasn't an invasive perusal. Raising his arms, he laced them behind his head. A casual grace filled his every movement.

"Of someone so interesting that even after nearly a fortnight, I'm still thinking of her. But after a few moments, it became clear that you're not her. Not even remotely like her."

God, the man was a genius at baiting her.

Naina looked up at him, a hot declaration dancing on the tip of her tongue.

It was me you kissed as if you couldn't get enough.

This was a cat-and-mouse game they were playing. A game she was insisting on. He knew she'd been the woman that night. She suddenly knew that he knew. Without a doubt.

Whatever lies she'd told herself not an hour ago didn't hold up now when the truth was shining in his eyes. When it was clear from the challenge in the tilt of his square jaw. When the air charged up every time they looked into each other's eyes.

So why had he hired her then?

To make sure she didn't sell her story to the media?

Or because he'd taken pity on her situation after she'd practically begged him to give her a job because she was so desperately in need of funds?

It had to be one or the other. And, more importantly, she had to be okay with either of those reasons. "Oh, I wouldn't dream for a second that I could hold your interest for even that long, Mr. Raawal. Now, shall we get on with the list of tasks still waiting for you?"

CHAPTER SIX

VIKRAM KNEW HE'D been very thoroughly and very politely steered toward work. Which should make him elated. One of them, at least, needed to keep their cool and focus on the job in hand. Needed to remember that there was no future in whatever this was between them.

But the hunger with which she'd watched his body, as if he were her favorite ice cream…the woman had no idea how obvious her expressions were. How artless she was in her desire.

He'd never particularly cared one way or the other that he had, as everyone stated, "stunning" looks. It had been an accident of a genetics pool contributed to by two of the most self-absorbed, destructive people he'd ever known. Yes, it had come in handy in his career. But it had only been one tool in a whole arsenal he'd been given to save his family from the huge hole his father had dug them into.

To save the prestigious Raawal name from becoming synonymous with scandal and shame.

But for the first time in his life, he found he was more than fond of his symmetrical features. More than happy to go through the rigorous exercise regimen his trainer had created.

Just because this woman looked at him as if she wanted to lick him up.

He pushed his fingers through his hair, a smile curving his mouth. He felt like a teenager, waiting to pass a note to the girl he liked. But without the burden of being the family's last saving grace.

For the first time in his life, he found a distinct pleasure in this chase. This attraction that was more than a simple need to slake his lust or scratch an itch. For the first time ever, he felt as if there was more to him too.

He was still smiling when she looked up from her notepad. Again, those eyes stayed on his mouth for a few seconds too long before they finally met his. "Why are you smiling?"

He shrugged.

Her mouth pursed. "As I've told you, I've already tackled the to-dos Rita had for next week. The remaining are a list of tasks I'm not sure how to deal with."

He nodded and pulled forward the tray of fruit the flight attendant had left him. "Did you catch up to Virat, Anya and Daadi like I asked before they left for the airport?" he said, reaching for a plump orange.

"Yes. I delivered the medicines she left behind. Although…"

"What?"

"Virat said you'd made me take an unnecessary trip across the city. He'd already picked up all of

Daadiji's medication from another medical store." She turned the pages back on the notepad. Her eyes danced with laughter when she found the page. "He made me note down a message for you."

"And?"

"And what?" she said, batting her eyelashes innocently.

"What's the message?"

"It's a little…colorful."

"You know you're dying to read it to me, Ms. Menon. So go ahead."

"He said, and I quote, 'My brother needs to get his interfering nose out of everyone else's business.' Anya then added, 'TBH, he really needs to get laid.'"

Vikram plopped the orange segment into his mouth. "Ah…what my brother and sister don't know is I've already taken their advice. Only…"

"Only what?" she demanded, suddenly all fire and sass.

Vikram blinked. "I'm sure you'd like nothing better than to hear salacious details about my sex life but I don't kiss and tell. Let me just say I'd have a hat trick record if this were cricket."

Her face lost all its color. "So you're boasting that you've had…" there was that pink along her cheeks again, "that you've been with three women in the last what? Month? Week? Day?"

He shrugged, thoroughly enjoying the overt displeasure on her face.

Jealousy had never looked so beautiful to his eyes before. He could practically see her launching herself at him, all fists and curses, demanding an explanation. And he would tell her the truth. That all he'd been able to think of was her. Her laughter, and her kisses and her eagerness and her hot mouth and her even hotter need. And then she would beg him to kiss her in that delicious throaty voice of hers and he would press her down into this very bed...

The sound of a page being ripped from the notepad made him look up. She balled the torn-out paper in her hand with a vicious energy that made him smile.

"Is something wrong, Ms. Menon? Are you thinking up a lecture for me again?"

She straightened her shoulders, but didn't meet his gaze. "No, it's your life. If jumping from woman to woman is what brings you happiness, then..." She ended it with a shrug.

But Vikram saw the disappointment in her face before she shielded those big eyes with her thick lashes.

She looked down at her notepad for a long time and Vikram let the silence build between them. Gave her the space to ask him if his boasts were really true.

To ask him if she'd just been one in a row of other women. To ask if he...

God, what was he doing with her?

He had no idea why he was egging her on like this. Yes, some of it was the fact that he absolutely didn't like that she seemed to have control of this thing between them. But some of it was also the fact that he didn't really know her. Or himself when he was with her.

Every look, every word, every exchange felt like a

thrilling ride. Leaving him either laughing at himself or her, or drowning in desire. Ever since he'd agreed to let her take Rita's job for the next four weeks, he'd been on tenterhooks the entire time.

Wondering if she would back out. Wondering what she'd do when she saw him again. Wondering if she...

The fact that he was turning into the cliché that he most abhorred—a cynical, hardened thirty-six-year-old man panting after an innocent woman more than a decade younger than himself, who to all intents and purposes didn't want anything to do with him in a personal way, which was the script of his father's most notorious scandal—still didn't stop his thoughts about Naina. Or the thrill he felt when she looked at him with just as much hunger as he did her.

When she looked back at him, her eyes were devoid of any expression. "Shall we start?" she said in that polite voice and he nodded. It was probably best she thought he was a bed-hopping playboy.

"Your father and mother called separately about nine times each. Rita told me that under no circumstance was I allowed to let them reach you until we looked over the subject of their calls first."

There was a question in her tone and Vikram answered it first. "She's right. Only Daadi, Virat, Anya, Zara, and now you...as well as Rita, of course, have access to my private number. It's not to be given out to anyone else. Including my parents."

Her eyes went wide. "Zara as in Zara Khan, the spectacular actress I adore who doesn't let anyone tell her how to live her life? The Zara Khan who's won three national awards, the Zara Khan who runs a shelter for abused women, that Zara Khan, right?"

"Yes. Zara's my oldest friend."

"I'll not do this to anyone else I meet but please, if we run into her over the next few weeks, will you introduce me? I'd love to ask for her autograph. I know it's childish but Zara's just amazing and I love her."

Zara was the most amazing woman he'd ever known. The one constant in his life. "It's not in the schedule but if she comes, yes, I'll introduce you, Ms. Menon." And since teasing her was like breathing, he said, "You don't want my autograph?"

"Not really," she said immediately, scrunching that adorable nose at him. "I've got what I want from you, Mr. Raawal."

The outrageously bold declaration made him tip back his head and laugh loudly. Vikram had to fist his hands at his sides or he'd be grabbing her with both hands and scaring the hell out of her. Desire was a tiger clawing under his skin. "What exactly is that, Ms. Menon?"

"This job," she said sweetly, challenge in her expression.

Ha! So the minx wanted to do battle, did she?

"So back to—"

"Anybody else who wants to contact me calls you on the line Rita gave to you. Every call needs to be—"

"Screened by me first. No one can reach you, yes, I know. Even if your mother's—"

"Even if my mother's screaming threats of destruction at you." He sighed. "Like I said, her penchant for drama pervades everything she says and does. But she doesn't have a vicious bone in her body."

"To be honest, I wasn't afraid of what Mrs. Raawal might do to me. I was worried more that she might find out that my stepmother is Jaya Pandit. Jaya Ma doesn't need any more bad luck and your mother's a woman of considerable influence in the industry."

"You have my word that no one will harm you or your loved ones in any way because of your…association with me." He cleared his throat. "It's important to me that you believe that, Ms. Menon. No actions of yours, past or future, will be used against you. I'd never abuse my position of power like that. If I fire you, it will be because you either violated the NDA you've signed or because you're not up to the job. Is that clear?"

The confusion in her eyes cleared. But she didn't look away. She didn't play coy. The truth of their night shimmered in her eyes. Along with her conviction in him. And the furor in his chest calmed at her absolute trust in him.

She looked back down at the list, though she remained quiet for a while. The silence lingered on, but it didn't rush at Vikram like it had done. It had a comforting quality to it now.

"So there's a woman who's contacted your mother who's claimed that she's…" She cleared her throat and tried again. "That she…"

Whatever pleasure he'd felt instantly siphoned out of Vikram, leaving only hardness behind. He popped another sliver of orange into his mouth but the sweetness felt like nothing on his tongue. He chewed and swallowed, forcing himself to speak. "Whatever it is, Ms. Menon, just say it. If you hesitate like this every time my father creates a new problem for me to solve, we'll get nothing done."

"Your mother has been receiving notes and calls from this anonymous woman claiming to be pregnant with your father's child. She said she's tried to deal with it on her own but hasn't succeeded."

"Is the woman demanding money?"

"Something like that, yes." She turned the page on the notepad and tapped her pen. "The gist of your father's messages was that he'd never met this lady before. At the time of…" She ran her fingers through her hair a couple of times, and Vikram watched bemused as it sprang back exactly as it had been before. "He pointed out that at what would have been the time of conception, he'd been in Paris with a different lady love of his. He also got pretty upset…"

"You're to hang up immediately if he's being—"

"He was drunk, I believe. Not aggressive. I couldn't hang up on him, Mr. Raawal. He sounded close to tears." She held up a palm, ordering him to be silent when he'd have interrupted again. "So I did call the hotel in Paris for confirmation he was with that other woman. I also crawled through that particular lady's social media account and while she doesn't come out and say she was with your father at the time, there's enough information to figure out that he's telling the truth. As per Rita's instructions for what to do in these scenarios, I passed on the blackmailer's information and all the other evidence I'd gathered to your lawyer. I mentioned it now just to keep you informed."

She didn't wait for him to say anything. He hated that he had to be grateful to her for the intense awkwardness. But then most of his adult life had been like this. "Shall we move on to the next thing?" she asked, still all business and he nodded.

"There's a report from your sister's PA that I'm to pass on to you." He heard the curiosity in her voice but she didn't indulge it. "There's a conflict between an awards show in Mumbai you promised to appear at and the charity youth program that you, Anya and Virat oversee in Delhi."

"Cancel my appearance at the awards show. I go to enough of the damned things; there's one in the Maldives while we're there."

She made a note, flipped through the notepad a few more times and made more notes on the two phones. "Those are the most important ones for now. Oh, and I heard from the retired actress you wanted on this project, Mrs. Saira Ahmed. She said, 'Tell your boss I'm not coming out of retirement just to help his self-indulgent, masala pop trash movie become a reality. His grandfather Vijay would be turning in his grave at what his grandson has done to his beloved production house.'"

Vikram sighed. There was no amount of money

or gifts that would change Mrs. Ahmed's mind. Damn it, he'd tried. He'd even hoped that throwing around Virat's name—after all, to the true artists among them, his brother was a better Raawal than he, might sway the stubborn old goat's mind. "That's that then."

"That's *not* that however," Naina piped up. "Rita told me how disappointed you'd be to hear Mrs. Ahmed's decision and so I tried something else."

He sat up, noting the glint of pride in her expression. She was practically vibrating with excitement and it tugged at Vikram. He wanted to shake her and demand she tell him immediately. He also wanted to grab her and kiss her hard as if he could fill himself with that joy of hers. "What did you try, Ms. Menon?" He forced himself to say her name formally, as if it could kill this constant need inside him.

"When I went into the city to drop off the medication for Daadiji, I dropped by this old library that Papa and I used to visit. The owner is this eighty-year-old man Chaudharyji with a private collection of books like you would not believe. Papa and he talked history for hours and he'd let me browse through his collection. I asked him to let me borrow the first edition of a poetry collection that Mrs. Ahmed's father wrote in 1935. I remembered seeing a feature on TV about how most of their possessions had been destroyed during the migration after independence. She was close to tears.

"I took the edition to her, and told her you went to a lot of effort to locate it and borrow it for her. I cannot describe her joy when she held that old edition in her hands. She hugged me and said it was clear that you had more sense than she'd previously credited you with if you had someone like me work for you, so," she took a deep breath, her eyes twinkling, "she said she will give you one chance. The script, she said, will have to be magnificent. I sat down with her secretary, hashed out some dates and she wants a look at the script in four weeks."

Vikram didn't, couldn't, say anything for long minutes.

She looked up and smiled. "Thank you—that's the phrase you're looking for."

He smiled. "Thank you, Ms. Menon. It's been my dream to have Mrs. Ahmed on this project and you brought us a chance. Now, is that all?"

"I called the resort and changed one of the reservations. Mr. and Mrs. Sharma would prefer to be in separate villas. The only member I haven't heard back from so far is Virat."

She closed the notepad and sighed. "Can I ask why you've gathered them all here? They seem like a very…"

"Eccentric, self-centered bunch of old has-beens?"

She smiled. "Those are your words. I was going to say interesting group of people."

"I've been trying to pin down a script for more than two years. Usually, Raawal House will just buy a spec script but this is close to my—" he cleared his throat, as if he couldn't admit that he had a heart or that it felt things "—that's important to me. There's a skeleton script ready but it needs fleshing out. And this bunch of self-important snobs are who I need to do it. But it's a pain to get them to work together.

"This is my last attempt at bringing this project to fruition, which is why we're holed up here in such stunning surroundings. I also have no doubt it's the reason Virat is MIA. He absolutely doesn't believe in coddling anyone or pandering to anyone's superiority complex. He'll turn up to contribute eventually, either in person or via video link."

"So it's a project you're going to take on together? You as lead actor, he to direct it?"

"Yes."

"To be released in time for the seventieth anniversary celebrations of Raawal House, right?"

"You're very quick, Ms. Menon."

"Yeah, we can often surprise you like that, us women."

"Ahh...still getting those hits in whenever you can, I see."

She clapped her hands together, the excitement on her face contagious. "This is amazing. I adore everything Virat has ever made. I can't believe you've never worked together before. I mean, you've both had unprecedented successes with everything you've ever touched."

"Like you, my brother thinks I'm a populist sellout."

"I never said that. I just..." She colored, and he decided to take pity on her.

"We need this group to produce what they're capable of, Ms. Menon. It's just a matter of getting them to communicate together. With Mrs. Ahmed wanting a look at the script, you know now what's on the line. I should have a history expert here, too, but the professor had an accident not two days ago."

"I have a master's degree in history and theater, and history of theater in India. Of course, I didn't get to finish my PhD in film history but that's all I've ever studied. I can help with anything in that area."

"It's all hands on deck at this point. I need a script of some sort at the end of four weeks, if I want to keep the investors I've attracted."

"What's the subject?"

"It's a biopic about my grandfather Vijay Raawal. With India's Independence struggle as the background."

"Oh, my," Naina said, dropping onto the bed. "The scope of it, the history of it…wow…just wow! That sounds magnificent. I can't believe I'm here to see its inception, to see history in the making.

"I mean, can you imagine? The struggles he had to face, the traveling theater stories, the increasingly charged atmosphere…" She suddenly looked at him, her heart in her eyes. "Will you be playing him?"

"That's the idea."

"That's…that's the role of a lifetime. And I have no doubt you'll be absolutely fantastic at it, Mr. Raawal. With Virat in the director's chair, the industry will see what you're really made of."

"Thank you for the vote of confidence, Ms. Menon. I wish my brother had the same confidence in me as you do."

His husky whisper in her ear made Naina realize, that in all her excitement, she had got really close to him on the bed. The arc of heat between them was instantaneous. All-consuming. All the excitement about the project seemed to have found new sources inside both him and her.

There was a stillness to him that felt like it was tearing at the edges. As if it were a deceptive front and one word from her would fracture his façade. This close, she could see the slight curl to his hair, helped along by the moisture of the recent downpour. She wanted to reach out and push it back, and keep her fingers there.

Her gaze drifted to his mouth, as if it were her true north. As if she could still feel the soft, hot weight of his lips on hers. She could vividly remember the corded strength in his thighs, the rough dig of his fingers into her hips.

The sounds he'd made when he'd climaxed inside her... The memories all beat through her with a tempting force that shook her. In that minute, all she wanted was to climb fully onto the bed, push him back against the covers and beg him to kiss her again. To make love to her again. To make her feel as if she was the most desperately needed woman in the entire universe.

But she couldn't.

Because he was her boss and she didn't want to mess up this job. She was only just discovering how much she wanted to work in the film industry. And while she believed that he'd never harm her reputation or prospects in any way, a relationship between them had nowhere to go, except to crash and burn. He wasn't a man who wanted marriage and babies and all the things she wanted.

There was no future for her with him.

Yes, Vikram Raawal was not the egotistic, privileged, arrogant ass she'd thought him at their first meeting. But he was still the superstar who had the reputation of breaking women's hearts. The confirmed bachelor. The control freak. The man who absolutely didn't believe in love or marriage.

But of course, she was tempted. She was more than tempted. With him, she'd been bold, beautiful, brazen even. She'd been a different Naina. She'd been a Naina she was proud of. But that Naina existed only in darkness and disguises. He was absolutely right about that.

Slowly, feeling as if she couldn't trust her own limbs to follow her commands, she got up from the bed and walked toward the front cabin. "I can't tell you how much this opportunity means to me, Mr. Raawal. I wouldn't do anything that would jeopardize this. Not for anything."

She didn't wait to see if he understood. This thing between them…would just have to fizzle out. It had to stay a fantasy.

CHAPTER SEVEN

EVEN AFTER TEN days, Naina still wasn't used to the magical splendor of the island. She had never seen a blue like that of the ocean before. The small island was tiny with one main resort building in the middle and cozy two-bedroom villas interspersed around. Crystal-blue water floated as tiny wood walkways connected the villas and the main resort as if they were glinting sapphires on a beautiful necklace.

Though working sixteen to seventeen hours a day keeping up with the supercharged life of Vikram Raawal meant she'd barely had the chance to do anything more than take a quick glance at the stunning beauty around her.

Fifteen minutes during every morning's catered breakfast—which was a veritable feast of North Indian, Continental and South Indian delicacies—sitting atop the veranda with a view of blue lagoons was still more than enough to fill her with a quiet sense of well-being she hadn't had in a long time.

Lunch, an informal buffet served at the main villa, was usually a working affair. During dinner, the team often dispersed and she'd gotten into the habit of bringing something to her room to eat while she finished up the day's communication.

She was sharing a villa with Vikram and the first morning, her main concern had been about stepping into the kitchen area and running into Vikram and his sexy masculinity before she'd even had the chance to have a cup of coffee. But by the time she'd showered and ventured out, he'd already left for the main villa. However late Naina stayed up during the evening, typing up notes, scheduling meetings and video calls for the next day, he worked later than her.

The team worked at the main villa with two bedrooms designated as workspaces for Vikram and Virat, who was still not here in person, although he had video-called several times. Vikram read the script nightly after Naina sent it to him and discussed revisions with the team first thing in the morning.

Despite the rift between them, the brothers were clearly committed to the project. She loved watching the arguments and discussions amongst the team about the main plot, dialogue and the two main characters, while Vikram played the referee.

Outside of the script, there were casting sheets to go through, video conferences with potential investors, sketches he oversaw with Ajay, and they were also combing through an incredible amount of research each evening.

They'd had Chaudaryji and Mrs. Ahmed on two conference calls—informal, sprawling discussions about that time period. Naina loved those calls—

even Vikram seemed to light up from within at the long, leisurely walk down memory lane.

Naina followed Vikram into the open lounge area after one such call, pulled toward him despite every rational voice that warned her differently. They'd finished early today, and twilight bathed the open lounge area with a grayish-blue tinge. With the soft swish of the water and a balmy breeze, the quiet had an otherworldly feel to it.

Fingers laced through each other behind his back, he was standing at the balcony looking out into the deep blue expanse of the ocean. The white linen shirt fluttered up in the breeze, baring the hard slab of his lower back muscles. Her fingers itched to touch him, her body suddenly flush with that cocktail of thrill and need whenever she was near him.

Naina couldn't help wondering at how greedy she became when it was him. True to their unspoken truce, they had both been nothing but professional in both their words and looks. And yet, the silence between them possessed a strange quality—as if it was hungry for words, tinged with anticipation.

Waiting and wanting.

This attraction to him, it hungrily ate up any rational excuses she threw at it.

She knew she should retire for the evening. If she hurried, she could join the rest of the team on their hunt for a nightclub. And yet she stood rooted to the spot. No luxury experience, no celeb spotting, nothing, she was beginning to understand, would hold more appeal than a simple, quiet conversation with this complex man.

Telling herself she'd already had her once-in-a-lifetime fantasy night with him, warning herself that this job was too important to jeopardize...nothing was helping. All her life, she'd carefully lived within the confines of others' expectations and now...now it was as if everything within her was rebelling against taking a sensible course of action. Everything in her, selfishly, wanted him. More of him.

She must slowly be going crazy, because she easily convinced herself that he needed her too.

Naina joined him at the small balcony, leaving enough distance between them just to prove she could.

Vikram cast her a look of surprise. Those eyes didn't miss the distance she'd put between them. His mouth twitched. "Not into the club scene?"

"I'm not into it, no, and Ajay's working late anyway," she replied, somehow managing to sound rational.

He frowned.

She wondered if he found her company that distasteful. "I didn't mean to intrude. I'll say goodnight—"

"Stay, Ms. Menon."

She bristled at the way he invoked her last name. As if it was an incantation that immediately imposed distance between them.

"You were in a bit of a strange mood earlier tonight. On the call with Mrs. Ahmed," she said, as if it was the reason she had sought him out.

He held her gaze and again, she knew she was just finding excuses to be near him. Even that knowledge didn't send her on her way. He sighed and looked back at the ocean. "I'd forgotten that little tidbit she mentioned. That Daadu had been rejected at least fourteen times before he got his first role."

"You miss him," she said, full of a giddy relief that he was talking to her. That he was sharing a private moment with her. That despite the game they were playing, he still considered her close to him.

God, she was going mad, if him just talking to her was making her this happy.

"I never got to know him that well before he died. All I remember is the rows he and my father would have, the disappointment in his eyes afterwards. One time, though, when things were really bad with my parents and I went to live with Daadu and Daadi for the summer, every night after dinner, we would lie on this handwoven cot in the courtyard, old *gazals* playing on the gramophone, look up at stars and he would tell me stories of brave kings and courageous queens and clever poets, and cunning spies in our history...he was a magnificent storyteller, with a true love for theater and cinema."

Just like that, everything that made this man into Vikram Raawal clicked into place for her. "I owe you an apology," she said, aware now that she'd deeply wounded him the first time they'd met. The shame of her judgmental words stung her.

Brows raised, he turned to her. Focused that intense gaze on her for the first time in days. "This should be good."

She shook her head at his lighthearted tone. "I was wrong. It's easy for the likes of Mrs. Ahmed and me to sit atop our judgmental horses and call you a sellout.

"But you never had the luxury to make the movies that met the vision of the company that your grandfather established. To simply take over and walk in his footsteps." She didn't have to mention the calls with his parents, the constant back-and-forth over finances, the better understanding she now had of his reign over the Raawals after only ten days. He constantly juggled a million responsibilities in addition to his own acting career and being the creative head of Raawal House. "You had to dig the production house from a financial hole really quickly, and then salvage its reputation when you took over. Have I got it right so far?"

He shrugged. "It wasn't simply the prestige of the company I was saving. Daadi would have lost her bungalow, the house Daadu built for her. We'd have lost the studio and gone into bankruptcy. So many livelihoods depended on me. All our employees— both at the studio and all the various mansions, they'd have been on the streets. Virat and Anya would've had to give up their higher education.

"My father sank all their personal fortunes into unwise investments and my mother lost hers on three huge movies that were supposed to give her career a second wind but then were major flops.

"They would have had to sell their cars and their mansions and everything. They'd have lost their entire way of life, and believe me, they wouldn't have survived it. They do not possess the strength of character to retire to simpler lives." She could still see the weight of that decision in his eyes.

"My first movie was my first and final gamble, with everything riding on it. I used everything I knew about mass appeal and made sure I created the most commercial blockbuster I could. And I never looked back."

"Why doesn't Virat get that?" she asked with a frown. "Why doesn't he understand that you've spent the last fifteen years of your career righting the mighty ship of Raawal House? What right does he have to call you a sellout when he's reaping the benefits?"

He studied her face with bemusement but she was far too gone. "Such anger on my behalf, Ms. Menon?"

"It's so unfair that you've carried this burden for so long."

"Virat simply thinks I should have walked away from the mess my father and mother created. That the prestige of the Raawal family didn't deserve to be preserved. Virat, you must understand, had a childhood that was eons different from mine. Mine was child's play compared to the…challenges both he and Anya faced with them, as they were quite a bit younger than me."

"Did you ever consider walking away? From the studio and your…family?"

"I did, for all of five minutes. But those long summer nights with my grandfather, the vision he had built into a reality with nothing but hard work, his love of family above all else…it didn't sit well with me. Walking away would have been cowardly."

"And you never regretted it?"

"Not the choice I made. For what it's worth, Raawal House stands as a symbol of one man's vision of cinema. My fortune is a hundred times what my grandfather ever made. If I say I regret building an empire and being rich, then I'm lying through my teeth. But…"

"But what?"

"Why such curiosity about all this, Ms. Menon?"

Heat claimed her cheeks. "I misjudged you. Some of it is the easy, casual cruelty with which we judge celebrities, delving into their private lives, standing on higher moral ground, combing through their every mistake, drawing satisfaction when they flounder. I honestly thought myself above all that.

"And some of it is just that I've come to…" Naina considered and rejected words that rose so easily to her lips, expressing feelings she wasn't ready to examine "…respect you. I feel as if I owe it to you."

"You don't owe me anything," he said, his gaze holding hers. For once, she didn't understand the look there.

"Then I owe it to myself, I think." Before he could analyze that, she said, "What do you regret?" In that moment more than any others, she wanted to call him Vikram. She wanted the feeling of intimacy it would give them, she wanted the right to demand answers from him.

She wanted...so much she couldn't even put it all into words.

He combed his fingers through his hair, his shoulders tense. "Not regrets so much as niggles. Certain recent events...have made me realize that there are consequences to my actions that I hadn't foreseen."

"Like what?"

"Like the fact that taking control of everyone's lives to fix a sinking ship has turned me into a control freak who can't keep out of his family's personal business. Like the fact that I seem to have lost my soul somewhere along the way in the pursuit of wealth and security. Like the fact that I..." He rubbed a finger over his temple and then shook his head. As if deciding that those niggles weren't important. "I've become so arrogant that maybe I don't even know myself anymore."

"I'd venture that most of that arrogance is innate rather than a byproduct of all the problems you've had to fix," she offered lightly, her heart heavy at the remoteness of his expression.

"Touché, Ms. Menon," he said with a laugh. "Guess you think you know me very well now, huh?"

She said nothing, suddenly finding her breath far too shallow under his intent gaze.

"I'm too practical to pine over a future that never really existed for me," he said finally. "Virat is the genius, the thinker who lives in alternate story lines and potential futures. I'm a hardheaded business-man. When you've had to make decisions for ev-eryone, life-changing decisions at such an age as I did, it becomes a deeply ingrained habit. It becomes a part of you—that controlling nature, the arrogant assumption that you know best for everyone. You stop listening to anyone, you think yourself invinci-ble. You...become distant from your family friends, maybe even your own heart."

"But if you have this self-awareness now, if you know that you need to bend sometimes..."

Naina heard the self-deprecation in his laugh. How had she ever thought this man a one-dimensional cardboard cutout?

"Knowing that I've become a controlling, arro-gant man is no help when it comes to changing, Ms. Menon. Most of the time, I think I'm too set in my ways to even want to change.

"Would you walk away from your stepmother and your stepsister even though they demand and take without a thought to your own happiness?"

She reared back from that softly worded com-ment as if it was a slap. "I told you. They're not bur-dens. They're..." She smiled once the sudden burst of anger died down. "This is what you've been talk-ing about, isn't it? This knowing what's best for ev-eryone. This belief in your own superiority? This is why Virat and Anya are often angry with you."

He shrugged.

"Tell me then," she demanded. "Tell me your opinion of my family. Of me. Of how I should be fixing my life."

"No, Ms. Menon," he replied calmly but with a hint of steel in his tone. "I've just crawled back into your good graces. I should like to stay there. Especially since we do make a rather spectacular team."

She preened at the praise. And she knew she should heed his warning. But a desperate need to know what he thought of her took hold of her. A self-indulgent yearning for his regard. "I'm a big girl, Mr. Raawal, I can take it," she said, mimicking his words from that first day. "Do your worst."

"You'll not like me for it," he said, coming closer. And then, he sighed. "Why? Why are you so bent on hearing what I think of you?"

"Let's just say curiosity is my number one sin."

"You never got over your mother abandoning you as a child. And to be honest, maybe it's not a thing one ever gets over. Add to that a father who at best sounds like the absentminded, messed-up sort, at worst, a man who should've paid more attention to his little girl instead of his own feelings of loss and devastation, and you had to grow up too fast.

"I know how that feels. I know what it means to have to take hold of the family reins when you don't even understand yourself. Only our innate natures are such that it appears I have to control everything and everyone around me and you..."

"I...what?"

"You…you make yourself indispensable to everyone in your orbit. You're afraid that if you don't move everything to not only anticipate what your stepmother and stepsister need, but lay it at their feet, they will abandon you too. That they will stop loving you."

"And what is it that you think I should do to fix it?" she demanded, thrusting her face into his, so angry that tears filled her eyes. "Cut them out of my life? I'm not like you. I can't screen my family's calls. I couldn't bear it if they were mad at me. I couldn't…" And just like that, she confirmed everything he'd said about her.

He came closer then, his fingers reaching for her face. Even knowing that she should jerk away from his touch, Naina didn't move. He'd given her enough time to retreat from him. He clasped her jaw with such reverence that something inside her burst open.

She wanted to crawl into his arms and weep. She wanted to beg him to hold her so tight that she didn't have to acknowledge the painful truth in his words. She wanted so much from a man who could dispassionately arrange his own life to mitigate emotional pain.

"Remember that I said it is one thing to know one's weaknesses and a whole other thing to actually do something about them?" His smile was all teeth and no real warmth. "I never said you should give them up, Ms. Menon. Only that you shouldn't let them hurt you.

"Why leave yourself vulnerable to people who

have a high chance of hurting you? Why not protect yourself?"

"How would you do it then? Draw boundaries around what they're allowed to do? Create rules for them to follow? I can't live like that." She wanted to walk away from him then because she was angry with him. Angry with herself. "Keeping everyone out, being cold and calculating like you are, loneliness eating away at me. Isolated from both joy and pain, with nothing to show for my life but material success and wealth and mansions," she practically yelled at him, fury and pain stealing away any rational sense.

She froze, disgusted and astonished with herself in equal measures.

Bracing for him to either cut her down to size or to laugh and tell her he didn't need her pity because lonely was the last thing he was. She wasn't even sure it was true. Only an impression she'd formed of him. Mostly full of delusion, maybe.

He simply stood there, without blinking, staring at her, waiting for the storm that was her temper to pass. As if he were one of the tall palm trees that bent and swayed during tornados but never broke.

After what felt like an eternity, he said, "Are you less lonely than I am, Ms. Menon? Truly not hurt by your stepsister's selfishness, your stepmother's thoughtlessness? Lie to me all you want, but I thought you weren't the kind to lie to yourself."

With that simple, softly spoken question, he made

her look at herself. At all her patterns and behaviors. At her dreams and fears.

"You don't have to take my word as law, Ms. Menon," he said, when she just looked at him, still hurt and angry.

His voice was full of a gentleness that felt like a lash against her skin.

His gaze did one final sweep of her, from her tear-filled eyes to her trembling mouth. When his eyes met hers, the look of resignation was so absolute that she wanted to beg him to not shut her out. "My obligation to you as your employer doesn't stretch that far. And beyond the basic courtesy, I don't have a personal concern in your well-being.

"Believe me, I have enough messed-up people to take care of."

And just like that, she was reminded, not undeservedly, that she was only his employee. He left before she could offer him an apology.

She'd offered him an apology for an earlier insult and had then immediately committed a new offense against him. But it was only with him that she lost her usually placid temper.

Only him who from the first moment of meeting her had challenged all her own beliefs and made her reexamine everything in her life. And every time he did that, she ended up not liking what she discovered.

CHAPTER EIGHT

COLD AND CALCULATING...

She'd made it clear what she thought of him when she'd told him that a few days ago. It wasn't as if Vikram didn't already know that about himself. But it had never bothered him this much before, like a shard of wood stuck under his skin.

She'd also proved that she was no match for him, for all that she boldly bandied words with him. Not when he didn't temper his words or his personality. He'd hurt her. Especially when she'd sought him out in the first place so she could express her concern at his restlessness.

Damn it, what did the woman want from him? Why did she look at him with those big eyes in which he could clearly read longing and desire and hurt? Why didn't she stay away?

Because that's what he was trying his damnedest to do.

He hated this obsession with her, that was slowly but surely spiraling out of control.

It wasn't as if he could have a fling with her and work her out of his system. For one thing, she worked for him. He absolutely wasn't going to engage in some torrid affair with an employee and then throw her away like his father had done several times over. For another, she was…no sophisticate who knew the name of the game.

She was the kind of girl around whom epic love stories were written. And he wasn't a hero on his very best day.

So, the last thing he needed to do was to seek her out.

But ever since Mrs. Sharma had pointed out that Naina had missed the team dinner he'd organized this evening, he hadn't been able to focus. It was strange enough that she'd deviate from anything he asked of her professionally.

She usually made it a point of retiring to her room long before he returned to their villa and it was already past eleven. Once he found her bedroom empty, there was no stopping him.

He walked out of their villa, already a strange thrill gripping him with each step. Why was it that even a confrontation with the woman held more appeal than a night of hard sex with someone else?

He would be professional if it killed him. He would keep his distance from her even if it was the hardest thing he'd ever had to do.

Because there was no way he could have Naina in his life. Not with the way he was wired and definitely not with the way she seemed to weave people into the very fabric of her life with such unconscious ease.

Which meant, this madness, this obsession with her, had to end.

* * *

Naina was sitting with her back to Ajay's side, her legs dangling over the armrest of the sofa, in the open lounge of the main villa, while he was sketching on his pad. He was one of those people who didn't fill every minute with unnecessary chatter and she loved seeing the sets and the costumes come to life from his clever fingers.

The huge plasma screen was playing Vikram's second movie, in which he'd played two different roles—of father and son.

Ajay, she knew, was watching it for research. She was watching it because she was…fixated on the man. There was no avoiding the fact anymore that all she thought of was Vikram.

Of how to be that bold Naina with him again, even if it was for just a night, a day, a week. Of how to have him, for herself, just one more time.

She knew she owed him another apology. And yet, if she sought him out for such a personal discussion again, she was afraid of what she might say. Of what she might do and demand of him.

So she was avoiding him. Which was a joke since she worked so many hours each day next to him. She felt as if she was standing on the cusp of something vast and important. As if something inside of her was changing and she didn't even know if she wanted to stop it. Or maybe it was already far too late to do so.

The younger Vikram on the screen took off his shirt and was doused with colored water in a Holi celebration. Naina sighed.

Ajay laughed, and pulled at the messy braid she'd caged her wild hair into. But his concentration was unbroken. She liked sitting by him when he sketched because he never tried to poke his nose into her thoughts. His rapidly moving fingers on the page sent vibrations up his arm and into her back. She stared at the emerging picture of Vikram—the sharp bridge of his nose, the deep-set, soulful eyes, the high forehead, and the mouth that could be languid and sexy in one breath and hard and calculating the next.

"You've got the lower lip all wrong," she said, when Ajay made it too flat. Too thin. Too…cynical. "It's much more…forgiving." She bent down and traced her finger along that lower lip, making it wider, thicker. "You also missed the crease he gets here when he smiles. You've made him far too brooding, too…"

"That's the man I see every day," Ajay said, his tone matter-of-fact.

"That's only one version of him. There's so much more to him than you…"

Ajay's fingers stilled on the paper. The sudden tension in his lanky shoulders transferred to Naina and she looked up.

Vikram stood just inside the doorway of the expansive lounge, looking down that arrogant nose of his at them. And he was angry. She didn't know how she knew that but she did. She quickly did a runthrough of all her to-do items in her head. No, she hadn't missed anything.

Ajay turned off the television and stood up, as if he'd been caught doing something inappropriate. Naina fell onto the sofa with a soft thud. Feeling like the most ungainly creature ever, she pushed herself up and into a sitting position, her skin prickling under the intensity of Vikram's scrutiny.

She'd never been so aware of every inch of her own skin—from the breeze kissing her bare legs, the embroidered hem of her loose shorts against her thighs, to the silk of her pink sleeveless chiffon blouse fluttering against her skin.

She felt as if he'd run those long fingers over every inch of her in that thorough way of his.

"Hello, Mr. Raawal. Did you need anything?" Ajay prompted, his spine ramrod-straight.

Naina refused to stand to attention. Refused to let him make her feel guilty. But her heart sped off anyway as she wondered just how much he'd heard her singing praises of his lower lip.

Vikram's gaze didn't shift to Ajay, not even for a second. "If I could borrow my assistant for a few minutes?" Politeness oozed from his every word as he held open the door.

Ajay picked up his sketch pad and pencils and disappeared under Vikram's outstretched arm, the coward.

Naina stood up as Vikram closed the door behind Ajay and ventured in. She hated it when he looked down at her from his great height. The light brown shirt and beige-colored khakis did wonders for his broad-shouldered frame and long legs. He looked effortlessly sexy in even casual clothes.

For long moments, he just stared at her face. It made her feel anything but uncomfortable. Already, during the time they'd been here, she'd become entirely familiar with how he weighed each word before he spoke, how he studied every nuance in his audience.

"I don't think I've ever seen you in anything outside of your usual colorful skirts, Ms. Menon. Maybe once. Definitely once."

Heat flared across her skin, the memory hitting her right in her lower belly. As strongly as if they were back in that darkened library, their fingers and mouths communicating for them.

She pulled the loose strap of her blouse back into place. His gaze followed her every movement, every breath until she felt like she was one giant string of tightly tuned need. One touch from him and she would burst into…ecstasy.

"It was too hot earlier. I…" Naina had no idea what was going on inside his head. "Is there something I can do for you?" she prompted, and then wished she'd worded it differently.

But he didn't notice. There was a strange tension in his face.

"Why weren't you at the team dinner?"

"I didn't realize it was mandatory," she retorted, defensive rather than defiant.

His gaze roved over her. "Are you unwell?"

He knew she was not. Even with the busy workload, the island and the schedule had done wonders for her. For the first time in months, she didn't feel weighed down by grief or fear. She'd never looked as good as she did now.

"Mrs. Sharma said you had a headache."

"Oh, that. I made it up when it looked like she would stay back with me. She's sweet but I didn't feel like company."

Naina watched in bewilderment as he pushed off from the wall, sauntered closer and picked up a sheet of paper at her feet. It must have come loose from Ajay's sketch pad.

Shock rooted her as she looked at the sketch. She hadn't realized Ajay had drawn her too. He had rendered it with his usual artistic brilliance, capturing such intimate details for a black-and-white sketch.

Her mouth was curved into a tentative smile, her hair its usual mess. But her eyes and mouth...he'd caught the wistfulness and the longing and the desperation with such crystal-clear clarity that she felt exposed, raw. As if things about herself even she didn't fully understand had been captured on paper for all the world to see.

She reached out to grab it. Her hand landed on Vikram's arm as he held the paper out of reach. Taut muscles clenched under her fingers, the side of him hard and warm against her front. Her breath became shallow as she realized how close they were standing. If she moved her head one inch, she could kiss his stubbled chin. If she leaned forward, her chest would graze his.

His harsh exhale was a warm stroke against her cheek. Her tummy began a slow roll as their gazes held, a million questions ping-ponging between them.

Naina knew in that moment what Ajay had seen with his artist's eye even before she had.

She would do anything if it meant she could touch, hold, kiss this man with the sort of freedom she'd had that night at the ball. And the depth of her longing went beyond physical attraction, beyond the need to be the center of his attention. So much beyond the powerful prize he represented.

She pulled away, sudden fear making her jerky.

Vikram's expression shuttered, the earlier tension swathing his frame again. "But Ajay was here with you. So it's only certain company you wanted to avoid."

Still too shaken, Naina couldn't summon the energy to rise to the bait. She felt as if she'd simply unravel if he said one wrong word. "Mrs. Sharma chatters constantly. Ajay missed the dinner because he had a call with Virat. I jotted down notes for him. Virat was in one of his brilliant moods..." She rubbed her temple, feeling a real headache setting in. "I'm sorry I didn't realize that the team dinner tonight was so important."

He stepped back. Naina had a feeling he'd come to some sort of decision. About her?

When he spoke, he was all formality. "Zara's flying in first thing tomorrow morning and seeing as she's coming, I've asked her if she'll do a photoshoot with me. She'll join us all at the resort afterwards. Tell the team they're free for a couple of days."

"I didn't know Ms. Khan was flying in. I'll let Virat know he can do her screen test. He said he might be here—"

"This isn't really a work trip for Zara," Vikram said, cutting her off. "She's mainly coming to see me. Virat and I haven't yet reached a consensus on whether she'll play the role of the prostitute spy yet."

"But she's perfect for the role. Virat doesn't approve of Ms. Khan?" she asked to keep the conversation going more than anything.

Thoughts swirled through her head like a whirlpool, sucking her in.

Why was the actress coming if not to join the project? Had Vikram specifically invited her? How long was she going to stay? Were they going to re-ignite their well-publicized on/off affair?

She wanted to demand answers from him even knowing that the answers might not be bearable.

"Virat and Zara have never seen eye to eye," he said, still staring at the sketch. "But I'll get my way in the end. See to the arrangements for her stay, will you? Clear my calendar."

"What about the call with—"

"Cancel everything for tomorrow and day after. You won't be needed either. Feel free to explore the islands with...the rest of them."

The command felt like a slap in the face. She couldn't help feeling as if she'd somehow failed him. "Wait, Mr. Raawal," she called out.

He turned, his expression even more closed off than usual. "Yes, Ms. Menon?"

"Did I do something wrong? Did I—?"

"No. You've been your delightful self, as always," he said with a smile that didn't reach his eyes.

It didn't feel like a compliment. She pointed to the paper in his hand. "Can I have that?"

He looked at the paper in his hand for long seconds. As if it was the most fascinating thing he'd ever seen. As if... Then he looked at her, his expression completely shuttered. "No. You may not," he said, and walked out.

Zara Khan arrived at the resort the next afternoon, straight from the morning photoshoot, arm in arm with Vikram. Naina would have given anything to hide, but the entire team had been determined to welcome the actress, their enthusiasm contagious.

She looked like an island queen in a two-piece yellow bikini and a bright white sarong wrapped around her waist as she walked over the wooden bridge, flanked by water all around, her beauty one of strong lines and angles rather than something that would fade with age.

In contrast to her extravagantly sunny look, Vikram was the perfect foil for her with his sculpted features and unshaven jaw. Dressed casually in khaki slacks and a white linen shirt rolled back at the sleeves, he was darkly sexy, his appeal a byproduct of his arrogance and power. That intensity of his presence, which was always a huge draw on the screen came from how deeply he felt about things. To call him cold and calculating had been unfair on so many levels, Naina knew.

She'd learned that the photoshoot was for an exposé that would feature Vikram and Zara as long-standing top Bollywood stars, their rise to stardom, their long-sustained careers, and their coming together for a behemoth project for the biggest project Raawal House had taken on in its seventy-year history.

At exactly the same time as the article ran, the sensational news about Vijay Raawal's biopic would also hit the industry.

Just because it was the project of his heart didn't mean it wasn't a huge, commercial machine that he was setting up to succeed at every level. With the knowledge of how many employees were involved, Naina was relieved that he was at the helm.

"So many livelihoods depended on me," he'd said, and she could see it in action now. But at the end of the day, she wanted to be the one he leaned on, for pleasure, for laughter. She wanted to be the person with whom he could be just Vikram. The strength of that feeling increased with every passing moment.

As the rest of the team surrounded them, Naina stayed back.

From a PR point, it was sheer brilliance to use the long-standing rumors about their possible romantic association to fuel the news cycle. Naina had never paid much attention to the gossip about them, but with them standing front of her right now, it was unavoidable.

Impossible to miss the ease and affection between them, to not see their gazes meet in wordless communication. Impossible to not notice that Zara Khan enjoyed a level of intimacy that Vikram didn't even allow his family.

Naina couldn't even hate her because the woman was graceful and down-to-earth when introduced to the team. Fresh fruit tasted like ash in her mouth when Naina returned to lunch.

Had he already lost interest in her then? Was it as simple as switching from her back to Zara?

Could Naina blame him when she'd made it so clear that she wanted nothing to do with him? When she continued with the pretense that night at the ball had been a one-off?

What would happen if she openly admitted to him that she was his Dream Girl? If she met him in the daylight as his equal? If she walked up to him and said, *I want more than a few hours of stolen kisses. I want to see where this will go. I want to make you laugh again like I did that night. I want you to kiss me again.*

What would happen if instead of doing what was safe, Naina reached out for what she really wanted?

CHAPTER NINE

CURSING HERSELF, NAINA picked up what felt like twenty pairs of earrings she'd thrown around the room when she heard someone come in.

"I'm almost done packing. You can start in the—"

"Where the hell do you think you're going?"

She straightened up to see Vikram and Zara standing at the entrance to her room. Damn it, she'd meant to leave before they returned from wherever they'd gone. For most of the afternoon and the evening. All seven hours of which she'd been acutely aware, down to the last minute.

Zara was dressed in a beautiful white pantsuit that made her look as if she'd just stepped off the pages of a magazine. Vikram, however, looked much more casual in a white linen shirt tucked loosely into blue jeans that hugged his lean hips and muscular thighs. He still hadn't shaved. He looked deliciously scruffy, but there was also a look of resolution in his eyes.

"Ms. Menon?"

Naina jerked her gaze to his. Barely banked impatience shimmered there. It made her own hackles rise. She'd waited all afternoon to approach him. To…take her chance. And he'd been…gone. With the woman who occupied the closest familiarity with him.

Jealousy was a vile taste on her tongue. She closed her fingers over the *jhumka* she was holding, the sharp metal of the earring digging into her palm. "I'm vacating the villa."

His jaw clenched. "Why?"

Naina busied her hands and her eyes with trying to close the zipper on her bag. "Ms. Khan and you will have more privacy here without my constant interruptions."

"You're a beast to throw the poor girl out, Vicky," Zara said softly.

"This is not on me, Zara. All I asked her to do was to make arrangements for your stay. Ms. Menon prides herself on anticipating every need anyone in this team might have and bends over backwards to fulfill them."

Naina dragged on the stuck zipper, fury rattling inside her. "You're the only member of the human race who thinks being nice to people is a serious character flaw."

"There's nice and then there's naive," he retorted.

She rounded on him. "Admit it, my 'innate goodness' that you sneer at so much is what finally healed the rift between Mr. and Mrs. Sharma and made them create that brilliant plot twist in the script. I'm the one who got Saira Ahmed to give this project another chance. I'm the one who—"

"No one's saying your contributions aren't valuable. But you don't even realize that half the team is taking advantage of you. You run their errands, you take notes for them, you…act as their champion to me and Virat. They've got you wrapped around their collective little finger."

"What's wrong with wanting to help?" Naina took a step toward him. "You've no idea how good I feel working on this project, working for you. Why is it that you're constantly—"

"Thank you for arranging that chat with Mrs. Ahmed. I've been a fan of hers for so long," Zara cut in, clearly jumping in to defuse an escalating situation. "Will you have dinner with me soon—tomorrow, perhaps? Or the following evening?"

"It was a small favor, Ms. Khan," Naina said, turning her attention to the woman studying her intently. If her heart wasn't in her throat, she'd have wondered what the gorgeous actress found *so* fascinating about her. "Dinner isn't necessary."

"I insist. I want you to come work for me, Ms. Menon."

"What?" Naina whispered, feeling as if the ground had just been stolen from underneath her.

"Vicky said he can spare you in as soon as three days."

Naina swallowed, keeping her gaze away from him. It felt as if he'd dealt a punch to her gut. "I… I can't accept your offer, generous as it is." She swallowed again. "Mr. Raawal's arrogance, as I'm sure you very well know, has no bounds. He likes to believe he knows me and my life better than I do myself."

Zara's mouth dropped open and then she laughed. The sound filled the stifling silence. "She definitely knows you well, Vicky."

To Vikram's angry gaze, it seemed no one but Naina existed. "You don't have to flee the villa in the middle of the night. As cold and calculating as I am, I don't throw my assistants out to sleep in the open."

"Ajay's okay with me bunking in his villa for the next week. Or until whenever it is that you're actually throwing me out."

"Like hell you're sharing with him," he declared, coming into the room and grabbing her bag.

"Why are you so angry with me?" Naina blurted out. "I should be the one who's... In fact, I *am* mad at you."

His head jerked back. "Go on, Ms. Menon. Don't get shy now."

Her skin prickled at his tone. "If this is about me calling you cold and calculating the other day—" Ms. Khan's stifled laughter filled the air "—I—"

"I don't want your bloody apologies."

"Then what *do you want* from me?"

"The truth." With one more stop, he came closer, the heat of his body singeing hers. "What will it take to get you to stop pretending?"

"Fine." Naina poked him in the chest, every emotion she'd been struggling to bury ever since that night they'd made love finally erupting out of her. "I'm leaving because from where I stand, it looks like the moment you lost interest in me, you invited *her*! I'm leaving because you know damn well it was me that night at the masked ball and I…want more. More of you and me."

Her face flamed as if someone had lit up lights under her very skin. Her fingers were shaking, her knees felt like pudding. And yet, Naina also felt as if a huge weight had been lifted. As if she had finally walked into the sunlight after stumbling around in the dark.

The tense silence that followed made her wish she could take a running jump into the ocean. Maybe swim her way across the Indian Ocean back to Mumbai. Or at least drown trying.

Vikram just looked as if he'd finally won the Best Actor award he kept being shunned for by the national film committee, every year. Now sitting on the bed, legs crossed at his ankles, mouth pressed into satisfaction, he was arrogance personified. She wanted to kick him as much as she wanted to kiss him.

Instead, she forced herself to make eye contact with Zara. This was not how she wanted to begin her associations in an industry in which she wanted to build her career. "I'm so sorry, Ms. Khan. I assure you I'm not usually so unprofessional."

"Oh, psshh…" Zara said, waving an airy hand. "This is the most fun I've had in a long while. I don't think I've seen Vicky jealous in…forever, actually. He's been terrible company the whole day. As for the villa, I'm afraid I was far too preoccupied with my own troubles to inform him before I arrived that I made my own accommodation reservations. Vicky and I don't need that kind of privacy, Ms. Menon. Forgive me for the confusion I created."

Naina didn't miss the nugget of information the actress had purposely offered. "I'll move out anyway," she said numbly, feeling like a fool.

"Zara, please leave us."

Vikram's quiet request cut through the tension like the crack of thunder split a calm, blue sky. Zara left without a word.

Naina's heart pounded in her chest as he got up and closed the door. She opened her mouth to speak but nothing came out. She swallowed and tried again. "I'm not leaving until the script is finalized. In fact, I've even figured out what Virat thinks is missing from it. I know how to—"

His soft curse exploded in the thick silence. "This is not about your job and if you were anyone else, you'd know it." He pushed his fingers roughly through his hair. "You fight me when I call you naïve, and yet you turn down Zara's job offer instantly?" His chest rattled with a sound that was half growl, half sigh. "God, you need a damned keeper."

Slowly, the full meaning of his words sank in. Of course, he was the one who'd recommended her to Zara. Why? To what end? Naina felt as if she was standing in a fog of unknowns—mostly created by her own feelings. But she had nothing to hide anymore.

"I don't want to work for her."

"Why not?"

"I don't want to be associated with anyone you know."

"That's most of the bloody industry then," he snarled, coming closer. Impatience etched into the lines around his mouth. He looked nothing like the suave, coldhearted businessman she'd called him that first day. "I won't have your joblessness on my conscience." He closed his eyes, sighed and then skewered her with his gaze. "Has it become so hard to be near me?"

"I don't need to be rescued. By you, especially." After months of being directionless, she knew what she wanted to do now. The last few weeks had filled her with a renewed purpose, with new zeal. Working with him on this concept had filled her with inspiration and energy. "Why are you so intent on kicking me off this project? Did I do such a bad job?"

"You've done a fantastic job of everything I've thrown at you. I just…can't have you working for me. Not anymore. It's too distracting.

"And FYI, you're selling yourself short if you think Zara's doing you a favor."

"And if I don't want to leave you?"

He raised a brow, and took in her resolute expression. She thought he'd ask her why she wanted to stay. It wasn't as if he hadn't stripped her to the core already.

She knew this was what being with him would mean. There would be no lies between them, no games, nowhere to hide, even if she wanted to.

There was something about him that brought out the boldest, best version of her and she loved being that Naina. Not a flicker of fear touched her.

He leaned back against the large window frame, his fingers wrapped tightly over the sill. "Why were you moving in with that…graphics guy?" he bit out.

"I don't want to move in with him so much as…" Naina looked at him, without her own emotions blinding her.

"It's been forever since I've seen Vicky jealous," Zara had said. He *was* jealous. Of her friendship with Ajay?

"You think I'm interested in Ajay?" she said, taken aback.

"Are you?" When she looked blankly at him, he sighed. "You've been spending a lot of time with him since we got here. Maybe you decided you've wasted enough of your life moping after your useless ex. Maybe you're making up for lost time, since you've discovered that men find you irresistible. Maybe you've decided you want more and more of those fantasy nights like the one we shared.

"I've been told by Virat and Anya and now Zara that I need to ask first and then act. So, I'm asking you first. Instead of just having him thrown off the project on some flimsy excuse."

"That's not funny, Vikram," she said, reaching for his folded arm. His muscles were taut under her fingers. "Promise me you won't do any such thing. You can't—"

He closed his other hand over hers, the contact

sending a shock wave of pleasure through her. His fingers were warm and tight over hers, and she wanted to lean into the touch even more. Until she was burrowed into his warmth. "That's what I need to do to get you to say my name? Threaten your latest boyfriend?"

"You've always been Vikram in my thoughts..."

Folding her arms, she gazed at him, the panicked thunder of her heart slowly settling down into calm acceptance. Standing here with him, discussing where this was going between them...shouldn't have felt so natural. But it did.

It felt easy and right and inevitable, since the second he'd walked into her room at his grandmother's house and asked her what was wrong.

"You won't fire Ajay," she said with confidence. "You're not the type to ruin a man's career because you're jealous. *If* you're jealous in the first place."

"Ahh...such faith in me, Naina?" He sighed, and this close, she could feel the tension in him. "Yes, I'm jealous. I spent the entire photoshoot imagining you being with him like you were yesterday evening. I was short with Zara for needing me right now. I've cursed Virat for recommending the guy in the first place.

"Then I cursed you for making me jealous. Every time, you called me Mr. Raawal, I wanted to drag you back into my bedroom and show you how familiar we are with each other.

"You've been driving me crazy, Dream Girl."

"I'm not interested in Ajay in that way. He's easy

to talk to. Maybe because he doesn't dictate what I should be doing with my life."

He groaned and turned away from her. "Are you going to hold that against me forever?"

"I don't know," she whispered softly, her pulse zigzagging through her entire body.

Forever...was that where he saw this thing between them going? Or was it just a slip of the tongue? Or his definition of forever could be completely different from hers. It could mean a week, a month. It could mean just tonight, could mean just long enough for them to reach climax.

And yet it didn't deter her one bit. Whatever he gave, for however long, she wanted it. She wanted him. And for the first time in her life, she was going to do precisely what she wanted. Take what she wanted.

She took a step forward and leaned her forehead onto his back, loving the solid feel of him so close. For long seconds, they stood like that, with just that small contact, their breaths tuning into the same rhythm. "Can I ask you something?" she whispered, before taking the final plunge.

His hands fisted by his sides and she felt his exhale as if it were her own.

"Ask away, Dream Girl."

Her smile felt like it came from her stomach, spread upward, filling her with indescribable joy. She was such a fool. Why had it taken her so long to reach out and ask for this familiarity? This intimacy? "You...you didn't invite Zara here because you're kick-starting your relationship with her?" She felt small, naïve, exactly the woman he called her asking that question, but she had to know.

"No. You know there's an awards show on the island coming up. She wasn't initially going to attend but I persuaded her to change her mind and come a few days early so we could do the photoshoot at the same time. Zara and I have no relationship to kickstart because we have never been involved like that."

"I'm sorry for assuming that you simply switched from me back to her."

He shook his head. "You're the only woman I've slept with for months, regardless of what I said to you on the flight here. But I'm not going to apologize for thinking you were with Ajay. It only says another man can also see what I see."

"Ahh...there's my old friend. Your mighty arrogance. Just when I think I couldn't like you any more, it shows up. Saving me from toppling headlong at your feet."

He turned his head, offering her his profile. "Let's hope you always think that."

Always and forever...she knew he didn't throw out words like that with everyone. He wasn't even that voluble with the general public. But neither was she going to build castles in the air. He clearly wanted her. For now. And that was enough for her, for however long it lasted.

The tight knot in her stomach was already melting, the sun-kissed scent of him coiling around her with a familiarity that comforted her, with a thrill that unraveled the twisted knot of her own emotions. She covered the last few inches of space between them and wound her arms around him. Solid and big and hard, he took her breath away. He made her excited and alive and she wanted to rub herself up against him.

She opened her mouth against his back, the thin linen shirt no barrier to the heat from his skin. She dug her teeth into the hard muscle. His grunt and filthy curse made her smile. "I'm distracted too. All I can think of is that I want a repeat of that night. A hundred repeats. Here. Now."

She didn't know when he turned. Or when he pulled her to him. Or how it was that he maneuvered them into the wide window nook and then she was atop him, her legs splayed across his lap with her arms around his neck.

All she knew was the jolting sensation of his mouth against hers. *Finally.* Of the heat and hardness of him enveloping her. Of the sweet, sharp taste of him reaching out into all her limbs like tendrils of magic.

Her rib cage expanded as if it couldn't hold her thumping heart, her blood sang. She moaned when he thrust his tongue into her mouth, and chased hers. When his big hands enveloped her waist and tugged her against him. When he groaned into her mouth when she licked him.

This kiss was nothing like the ones at the party. Those had been sweeter, exploratory, a benediction. She realized, panting now, how gentle he'd been with her that night. How much control he'd exerted, how much he'd let her set the pace. How much he had made it all about her. It had been an introduction to the pleasure he could weave using her own body. It had been soft and inviting and full of promises.

This kiss...was the exact opposite. This kiss simply took. With nips and bold strokes, this kiss claimed her. *He* claimed her. There was no leash on his hunger. No soft invitation to feast on him. No playing nice for the wide-eyed virgin. This time, he gave her his rough need, his desperate bites, his urgent, panting groans.

He licked and nipped and soothed, leaving no doubt as to how much he wanted her. How easily he could steal her breath and give her his own back.

He wasn't gentle with her—not his lips on hers, not his fingers on her hips, not his body when he flipped her over and lay her down on the bed against the fluffy cushions. And Naina loved it all. Loved that she'd brought him to this desperation with just her words.

He knelt over her, between her legs, his gaze drinking her in. "Can I touch you?"

He asked in such a quiet yet fierce voice that Naina shamelessly blurted out, "Yes, please." She licked her lips. "Sometimes I wonder if that evening was a dream."

"I do too. And I want to know so badly that it wasn't."

"Yes, please," she said again and he laughed.

"These shorts have been driving me crazy," he said, before yanking them down.

And then he made love to her with his fingers.

All Naina knew from the moment his fingers disappeared under the seam of her panties was pure pleasure. First soft and slow, like the wings of a butterfly, to deep and visceral, until she was chasing his hand in pursuit of the peak.

And through it all, he learned about her. Watching every expression on her face, listening to every gasp, asking her what felt better, what she wanted more of, what would push her over the edge.

By the time she was fragmenting into a thousand shards, Naina felt as he'd bound her to him permanently. She could imagine no other man showing her this care. No other man watching her with such ferocity. No other man putting her needs first.

Their foreheads leaning against each other's, their breaths were a harsh symphony. Her sex still pulsed from her orgasm but Naina wanted more already. She wanted everything. And she was beginning to realize that everything with this man could literally mean her...*everything*. Her mind, body and soul.

But even that stray thought couldn't dull the impulse to touch him. To know him. To learn what gave him just as much pleasure.

"You know what I regretted most about that night?"

His gaze jerked to her, his brows drawing into a scowl. "What?"

Pushing herself up onto her elbows, she snuck her

hands under his shirt. "That I hardly touched you at all. That I just lay back and let you...do all the work. Today, I want to rectify that."

"I will let you have your way with me. To an extent," he added.

Naina rolled her eyes at his arrogance, refusing to let him deny her this.

Warm, taut skin greeted her questing, hungry fingers. She traced the ridge of his abdominal muscles, up his defined pectorals. Some instinct she didn't even know she had made her alternately scrape her nails against the smooth skin and then pull through the rough trail of hair. Up and down, she ran her fingers.

Head thrown back, he let her have fun. Let her have her way with him. A profusion of joy and warmth filled her to see him submit to her this way. This all-powerful man to the entire world, and with her...he was Vikram. Just Vikram who liked old songs and tart retorts and rough kisses and her. He was this way only with her, and it was the biggest joy she'd ever known.

The corded muscles in his neck stood out. Pushing herself up even further, Naina pressed her open mouth against the hollow of his neck and licked him. His arm came around her waist immediately, holding her up while she feasted on the jut of his shoulders, the pulse at his neck. Always watching out for her.

His innate concern only twisted the hunger more tightly inside her. She wanted to crawl into his heart and burrow there. Clasping his cheeks with her palms, she sucked his plush lower lip into her mouth. "I told Ajay he was getting this curve of yours all wrong," she whispered.

He raised a brow.

"When he was drawing you," she clarified.

He still glared. And then he sighed.

"I don't want to hear his name right now, Dream Girl." He tugged at her lower lip with his teeth in retaliation and she moaned at the sharp sting. The sheer heaven of his caresses pulsed even brighter in contrast. He soothed the tiny hurt by blowing on it, his eyes raking over her face. "I don't want him drawing you anymore. That picture of you…it was brilliant. And it felt like he achieved that only because he knows you so well."

Her eyes wide, she stared at him. "You're serious."

He hummed his assent against the shell of her ear.

"I find I'm very possessive over you, Dream Girl. The fact that he laughs with you, that he shares his talent with you…that he knows you so well, while I watch on like a spectator, wanting so badly to be the one to be next to you…it's hard for me to reconcile at my age what a sore loser I am. So take pity on me and refrain from any more midnight trysts with him."

She giggled and traced the lines around his mouth. "You're not that old. And it wasn't a midnight tryst. We were watching one of your films. He idolizes you."

He simply shrugged. As if this didn't make a whole lot of difference. Suddenly serious, he cupped her cheek. "You're one of those people to whom everyone is drawn. I'm realizing that now. I was wrong to assume you're a pushover."

She plunged her fingers into his hair and sighed. "Ajay and I are just friends. We laugh a lot and—"

"Ah…there's the rub, Dream Girl. It's not that I don't trust you. It's just that I…"

"You're what?" she said when he trailed off, caught by the expression in his eyes. It was unreadable. Suddenly, it felt as if she couldn't reach him. As if he'd drawn himself behind a curtain she couldn't open.

"I'm selfish, especially it seems, when it comes to you. I don't want just your kisses and your moans. I want your tart comebacks, your hopes and fears, your laughter, your dreams…" Holding her gaze, he ran his big palm over her neck, to the valley between her breasts, to her belly and finally, to cup her mound. "…your everything." He pulled away, and she felt the loss of his touch like an ache. "I want you too much, this too much. And in my experience that's never a good thing."

"Speak for yourself," she said, not liking his tone or the bleak look in his eyes.

Determined to erase his sudden doubts, she slowly kissed his jaw. Dotted a line of open kisses to his mouth. This time, it was she that took. She who kissed and nipped and bit and licked until they were panting against each other. It was she who controlled his pleasure, she who chased his tongue in his mouth, she that became the aggressor. And she loved it.

She pulled his skin between her teeth, while sending her fingers back down, past the waistband of his trousers, to his throbbing erection. The hardness of him against her palm had her moaning out loud.

With a boldness she'd discovered she loved within herself, Naina scooted closer, until his thigh was pushing up against her core. She traced the shape of his shaft through his jeans, up and down, cupping and stroking, reveling in the tight tension that deepened in his body as she caressed him.

She had done this to him. Her.

"Inside me, please," she begged, beyond reason now. Beyond caring that Zara Khan or anyone else could walk in here and find them like this. All she wanted was to feel him inside her again. to experience his thick heat moving faster and harder, to hear him finding his ultimate pleasure with that hoarse grunt in his throat.

When her fingers reached for his zipper, his fingers tightened on her wrist. Stalling her. Stopping her.

"What are you doing?" she said, falling back onto the pillows, her tone sharp to cover the sudden shaft of fear.

Gaze lit with some unreadable emotion, he held her arms above her head. Bending down, he took her mouth in a rough tangle of a kiss that left her breathless but was in utter contrast to what he said next. "We should stop now."

She jerked her hands away from his grip. "Why?"

"I need a moment to…collect myself. A few days

to process this. It's the consequence of being a man of a certain age."

She widened her eyes, forcing humor into her tone. "Oh, you mean you might not be able to...perform?"

He nipped the lush mound of her palm and then soothed it with a kiss. "No, you minx." He sat back on the bed, his expression thoughtful. "Technically, you still work for me and I swore to myself a long time ago that I...would never repeat any of my father's actions, including sleeping with an employee. Not discounting the fact that any association with me of this kind will plaster your face everywhere in the media. I...have to think of the consequences first. To me. And to you."

"Is that why you recommended me to Zara?"

He shrugged, and she knew she wasn't going to get a complete answer. "You will do well working with Zara. Especially since the replacement for my assistant will start soon anyway. And yes, I thought a little distance might be good for both of us."

"Me leaving to work for Zara was a little distance?" she asked, fighting the dark cloud that seemed to come across them all of a sudden.

"I should apologize for not discussing it with you first, but it wouldn't be honest." He rubbed his jaw, his eyes shining with unspent desire. "You always throw a wrench in the works, Dream Girl."

"Is that bad?"

"Not all the time."

"Then what is it that you have to ponder?"

"One of us needs to keep an eye on where this is going and it should be me. We need to be very careful. I don't want to hurt you, Naina."

"You would never hurt me."

His eyes gleamed in the low light. "That kind of blind trust is…dangerous. No one's worth your trust, Naina. That's what I'm trying to tell you."

"You said you wanted truth. That is my truth. I trust you absolutely. I know I'm going to sound like a heroine in one of your movies with no life before you arrived on the screen. But… I was only half-alive before that night at the ball. The sun feels brighter on my face now, the world more colorful, even my own emotions are sharper and more defined… You helped me realize who I am, and what I want, Vikram. And you're what I want now."

The more she said to convince him that she wanted him, the more he seemed to retreat. He shook his head. "You're…"

She sat up and gathered the pillow to herself as if she could protect herself against what was coming. "I'm what? Help me understand."

"You're…*you*, Naina. Your honesty, your artlessness, your innocence, you…make this very complicated."

She felt as if he was listing everything about her that made her unsuitable for him. Unsuitable and gauche and…just not enough. Anger rescued her from pathetic hope, from begging him. "What the hell does that mean?"

His silence spoke for him. His eyes said everything.

"I've made hard decisions just like you did, at a young age. When Papa passed away and I realized our home was mortgaged to the hilt, I gave up my PhD to find work to pay it back. When Maya got sick and needed round-the-clock looking after for weeks, I did it. Even though it meant canceling plans with Rohan, plans we'd made for months.

"I have lived through disappointments and hurts and setbacks just as you have.

"You don't have to protect me. From the real world. From you. From this." Frustration made her growl. "Even when I didn't admit to you that I was Dream Girl, we've been honest with each other. Whether this thing between us lasts for one night or one week or one month, all you have to do is say it's over. I can take it."

"I know that."

And yet, he didn't make a move to touch her. Stubbornly kept his distance. It was clear that something was still eating away at him. Clear that even after all this honesty, after stripping her defenses from her, after making her drop her barriers and admit to so much, he still didn't consider her his equal. He didn't consider her good enough for his sphere, for him.

"I have to be the first woman in the universe who's being rejected because the man has principles," she threw out.

"This is not a rejection, Naina."

"No?" Naina stood up on trembling legs and gathered her dignity. Seeing that she had just humped his thigh like a dog in heat, it was a little hard. "Was it just a power trip then? Making me admit how much I wanted you, giving me that orgasm without letting me give you pleasure in return…was it all just to prove that you have this…power over me? To prove to yourself that you can win me from some other guy?"

He flinched and she felt a moment's satisfaction that she had wounded him. It was fleeting though, for it wasn't in her nature to hurt anyone. And she didn't want to hurt him, of all people. She wanted to be a part of his life for as long as he'd allow, and he was taking that away from her.

"You know me better than that, Naina," he finally said. Still not touching her. Still not moving.

"I thought so too. But I've been proven wrong before. Maybe you're right and I will always be a little too naïve and little too foolish when it comes to men."

He called her name as she left the room but she refused to listen to him and his great principles anymore. She wasn't going to cry over him. She wasn't.

She had gambled everything and she'd lost. That's all this was. That's all it had to be. And yet, she couldn't help but like the man a little more for sticking to his own damned rules.

CHAPTER TEN

NAINA WAS TYPING away at her laptop in her bedroom, with a steaming cup of chai and a plate of samosas, while the rest of the team got dressed for the awards show to which they'd all been given free passes, thanks to Vikram's generosity.

It would be a frivolous, fun evening but the last thing she wanted was to be reminded why she didn't belong in the same sphere as Vikram, to see him and Zara on display for the entire world to see.

It had been three days since their showdown. Three days in which Naina had stubbornly stayed. Because leaving would have meant running away and letting him win.

He'd wanted to simply remove her from her role as his assistant, supposedly to give him time to work out how to manage any personal relationship they might have. But the reality was, she would be out of sight, out of mind. Apparently, she could be just as bloodthirsty when it came to arrogant men who made executive decisions for her.

In the stark light of day, she'd even succeeded in

convincing herself that she'd had a fortunate escape. A man who could exert such self-control at that level, a man who could pull away that easily in the middle of lovemaking when he so badly wanted her—and Naina knew how desperately he'd wanted her...how could he ever feel comfortable with the strength of her emotions?

But when night fell and she heard him come into the villa long after she'd retired, when she heard his footsteps pause outside her room, when she remembered catching him looking at her as they worked, as if he couldn't get enough, when their hands touched innocently and lingered, she fell right back into the pit.

Fool that she was, she'd even deprived herself of Ajay's company. Not to pacify Vikram but because Ajay saw too much. The last thing she needed was to be pitied over Vikram's rejection of her.

It was his loss.

If she said that enough times in her head, she was going to believe it. Soon.

The silver lining however had been the camaraderie that built between her and Zara. True to Naina's first impression, the actress was down-to-earth and kind—mythical qualities in the industry. She had insisted Naina join her for her dinner last night, and just for that, she had all Naina's gratitude.

She had a feeling Zara knew most of what went down between her and Vikram. At dinner, she'd said, "The world is built for men to take it from us, Naina. Vicky is a good guy. But don't change, even for him. Don't let him take a single thing more than you're willing to give. Not your tears, not your joy, not your ambition."

"He doesn't want anything from me," Naina had replied, still smarting. "I'm not sophisticated enough to play his game."

Zara had squeezed her hand. "What is sophistication but a mask against hurt? You caught his interest because you're genuinely you. You can learn to play games but do you think we can all become a more honest version of ourselves, like you? Listen to your heart. You know him better than anyone."

"You're closer to him than anyone else. Even his family." Naina was ashamed to hear the hint of jealousy seep into her words.

Zara, the lovely woman that she was, just smiled. "We've been good friends for a long time, yes. But I've never seen him the way he is with you. You get to see the real Vikram, the Vikram even he doesn't know exists, methinks. And there's nothing more threatening to a powerful man than the unknown."

Naina didn't know what to make of that. Weighing it up, she thought Zara's insight might be useful. Naina wasn't a pushover, but Vikram had made her realize she could do a better job of establishing her own boundaries. Of giving her own wishes and dreams as much weight as she did Jaya Ma or Maya's. Of learning to love without fear.

She couldn't help seeing everything through the lens of his words now, herself included. She had always operated out of a worry that she'd disappoint everyone around her and that had to end.

This morning, she'd asked Zara if her job offer was still open and accepted it. Even in this, the blasted man had been right.

Why should Naina change the course of her whole life because of him? She resolved to speak to Jaya Ma about Papa's debts as soon as she returned home and persuade her that they should sell the house to pay them all off.

She'd clung to it only because she'd had memories of Mama and Papa living there. But Papa would never have wanted the house or his debts to become a millstone around her neck. To stop her from moving forward in life. Once again, Vikram had been right.

A knock sounded at her door. Naina opened it to see one of the staff members standing there with a luxury designer shopping bag hanging from her fingers. Before she could reply, the woman thrust the bag into Naina's fingers and left.

Shaking her head, Naina pulled out the contents of the bag. A beautiful pale yellow dress slithered out from between layers of expensive tissue paper. Her mouth falling open, Naina tentatively unfolded the gown. Weightless and silky, the long gown caressed her fingers, instantly lifting her mood. The corset had been embroidered with hundreds of beads and then the dress flared at the hips in a high-low hem.

On impulse, Naina held it against herself in front of the mirror. It would fit perfectly. She smiled at her reflection. Further inspection revealed no note but a velvet case that made her heart thump. She opened it to find an intricately twisted white gold necklace with delicate white stones that would glimmer against her skin.

Zara had already offered to lend her an outfit, although Naina had refused. She should've known Zara wouldn't simply leave it at that.

With the dress and jewelry in hand, she didn't even have the excuse of not having anything good enough to wear to hobnob with the A-listers.

She'd been prepared to have a fling with the sexiest Bollywood star in history three days ago. She'd even talked about the script ideas she had for the project with Zara just yesterday. After months of grieving for her father and having lost her way for a while, she'd finally found her stride.

She wasn't going to spend tonight moping in her room. It didn't matter if she wasn't good enough for Vikram Raawal.

She was good enough for herself.

He hadn't thought she would come. He had fiercely hoped though and that had been a distasteful experience. He'd never in his life hoped for someone else's actions to make his day better.

But then Naina had already changed so many things. Burned so many assumptions he'd lived with down to the ground. The challenge lay in understanding which emotions could be managed or willed away and what needed to be indulged, within the limits he set for himself.

From the moment he had seen her on the flight, laughing with Ajay, he'd known things were changing. Day after day, he'd been telling himself that this lingering…madness, because he still wasn't sure what to call it, over his innocent, too-good-to-be-true assistant would go away.

It hadn't. And to continue to lie to oneself was both foolish and dangerous. When he'd seen her late at night alone with Ajay, he'd realized that the time to do nothing had already passed. If he didn't act quickly, he would fall into a pit of his own making.

If he didn't take things into his control…his emotions would begin to rule him. His everyday life, from the smallest minutiae to the biggest decisions about family, career, even the house he lived in, would become ruled by his need for her. His entire life would be defined by how he felt rather than what he did, at the mercy of someone else's fickle emotions and that was unacceptable to him.

Not that he believed for one second that Naina was fickle.

I was only half-alive before that night at the ball… God, the woman had no idea how incredibly addictive her particular brand of honesty was. Of how easily she shackled him with those artless words. She wore her heart in her eyes and Vikram wanted it so badly. He wanted how she looked at him to last forever, he wanted to be the hero she thought he was.

He saw now what an utter disaster it would have been for Zara and him to get married. They'd never been attracted to one another and he could only thank God she'd had the sense to turn him down. It wouldn't have been the explosive minefield of his own parents' marriage, to be sure. But there also wouldn't have been an iota of challenge in it either. Not a single spark of this excitement he felt as he stood there just contemplating what Naina would say next.

Or do next.

He and Zara were too alike. Too controlling. Too used to having their own way to let anything exciting grow between them. Maybe even too flawed for life to be anything but another cycle of that rote existence that had been gnawing at him of late.

All he needed to do now was course correct. A marriage where his heart wasn't involved but his body was, where he was absolutely certain of his wife's loyalty and trust...that was the ideal solution for him. Naina was the answer he hadn't realized he needed. She made all the dissatisfaction, the lingering restlessness of the last year disappear like sunlight cutting through fog.

Admitting it to himself brought an intense relief shuddering through his body.

In just a few short weeks, she'd made him uncomfortably aware of how possessive he could be, of how much he wanted to rearrange her entire life and everyone revolving around her in their comfortable orbits, just so that she could never be hurt again. Of how much he wanted to protect her from the world, and sometimes even from herself. What better way to do it than to look after her for the rest of their lives?

He'd spent three days keeping his distance from her, weighing the odds and ends of the entire thing and finally reached a decision, a decision that would serve both of them well. Once he made up his mind, Vikram never regretted or second-guessed himself. Never looked back.

All that was left was to convince her.

He stayed behind a pillar and watched her as she flitted from group to group on Ajay's arm, looking like a beautiful butterfly.

The silky yellow dress was perfect for Naina's petite figure, and the diamonds at her throat only emphasized the sparkle in her eyes. He loved that she was wearing an outfit that he'd particularly chosen for her. It was an underhanded way of getting her to accept it, thinking it was from Zara rather than him, but he'd so wanted to spoil her. Wanted to give her everything she could ever want.

Even here, among so many beautiful people, there was something innately different about her. Something that snared his attention from the moment she walked in and held it. Not that he doubted his attraction to her, or the depth of his need for her.

She was his. Only his.

Naina was more than glad she'd come tonight. She'd thoroughly enjoyed the performances by some of the most noted Bollywood stars and musicians. Had laughed her heart out at one comedy skit that had satirized Vikram amongst other actors and actresses.

Naina had enjoyed drinking champagne that tasted like rainbows, eating delicacy after delicacy dripping in butter, dragging poor Ajay to the dance floor and shaking it up to some fast numbers.

She'd spotted Virat, who'd flown in for the show, and waved at him from a distance, not eager to impose. He'd walked over anyway and hugged her, genuine affection in his eyes. She'd even been a reluctant witness to the awkward tension when Virat and Zara had come face-to-face. Vikram must truly have the emotional range of a spoon if he thought these two simply didn't like each other. Naina felt as if she'd been standing in a minefield of unspoken words and longing.

Through all the excited gasps and unbelievable star sightings, she was aware of where Vikram was every single moment. Aware of her speeding pulse any time he was nearby.

It was supposed to have been only a fling if he'd agreed, wasn't it? And yet, she constantly felt as if she'd lost more than that. More than just laughter and the chance for some spectacular sex.

No. He had taken a part of her with him whether she'd been willing to give it or not.

The thought didn't bring the frantic fear she'd expected, however. Like she'd told him, she had lived through harder times. Meeting Vikram had only made her stronger and she would survive this too.

While most of the team were living it up and celeb-spotting as if their lives depended on it, Naina followed his every movement from when he'd showed up at the stage to announce an award to the edge of the dance floor later with a drink in hand.

It was hard to see him with Zara, touching her casually, cocking his head close when she whispered something, draping his arm around her waist for a photo op…

Now that she understood their relationship better, it was also clear that what Zara and he shared was affection, even love, yes. But not romantic love. Anyone with a little sense could see that but of course the press always wanted to speculate about the couple regardless.

The bungalow where the after-party was held had a lounge with floor-to-ceiling glass walls all around offering a spectacular view of the ocean, with people spilling out into the garden and the marquee. Small crowds huddled under the gazebo, in the upstairs balconies, and some lounged by the infinity pool. Lanterns placed artistically lit up pathways everywhere.

It was entirely a different sphere of life, and she'd recklessly tangled with the uncrowned king of it all. She smiled at the vain thought even as she saw more than one beautiful woman sidle up to him.

Having fun at the party while he was an out-of-her-league Bollywood star was one thing, but standing near him, knowing that she'd seen a part of him that no one else had, while he joined their team and complimented Mrs. Sharma on her pretty sari and teased Ajay on his awful dance movies…was quite another.

She both hoped he'd ignore her and prayed he wouldn't. The man was turning her into a certifiable mental case.

"You look lovely tonight, Ms. Menon," he said suddenly.

Six pair of eyes turned to her, as if to appraise the truthfulness of his comment. Her heart took a little tumble as his gaze found hers. "Thank you," she said primly, knowing from the glint in his eyes that this wasn't the simple kindness he'd offered everyone else. Which was in itself unusual. He wasn't the type to engage in casual chitchat with his team. Or anyone for that matter.

"That dress is quite different from your usual colorful skirts."

For a horrific second, she thought he was mocking her style.

She ran a hand over her belly nervously. "Yes." Something in his gaze made her spine stiffen. Why was she letting him drive this conversation? "But then, this isn't my usual playground, is it? I had to borrow pretty feathers to cover up my usual artless style and my far-too-honest mouth. It's been made very clear to me—"

"Ahh...so then that red lipstick isn't quite doing its job." His gaze flicked to her full, lush mouth for a second. "It certainly fooled me."

"That I'm not sophisticated enough," she finished lamely.

"While I love your usual colorful skirts and dangling *jhumkas*, I have to say you rock this look too. Not that I'm surprised."

Her pulse raced as she realized he was not being facetious. "Thank you."

"Who said you're not sophisticated enough?" Mrs. Sharma jumped to her defense like the mama bear she was.

Naina shrugged. "Never mind, Mrs. Sharma. It's

okay," she said, scooting closer to the other young guy on their team—a total idiot whom Naina usually avoided like the plague—and tangled her arm through his.

Two could play at this game. She would play so many games that Vikram would forget what artless and honest meant.

"I don't really have the taste for the high life. Too fickle for me. I'm happy where I belong."

The idiot took his chance and pulled her closer to his side, his muscled arm tight around her waist, smooshing her boob into his side. Naina thought she might throw up a little in her mouth.

Vikram on the other hand looked as if he wanted to separate the guy's arm from its socket. But such a vulgar display, she knew, was limited to his movies. Messy emotions had no place in his cultured, controlled existence.

But when he looked back at her, while the team saw their grumpy boss with a polite smile on his face, Naina saw something else. He hadn't succeeded in obliterating every emotion right then. His tight jaw, the way his teeth gripped his lower lip told her that.

"You clearly can move through worlds, Ms. Menon. Masked or unmasked, no man worth his salt could fail to recognize that you're the real thing."

Every word hit Naina like a fist to her heart, vibrating in her very cells.

If there was any doubt left among her team that this wasn't a usual interaction, that comment put paid to it. They stared in stunned disbelief at the raw, genuine emotion ringing in his words.

Did he want the team to gossip about them? Now, when she was on the verge of leaving? Why was he torturing her like this?

"Far too real then," she said, self-mockery filling her words. "And here I always thought I was not enough. Apparently, the opposite's the problem."

"Naina, *beta*, what in the world are you talking about?" Mrs. Sharma interrupted, her gaze swinging between her and Vikram.

Naina searched for something to say. "I think I will go thank Ms. Khan again. She was kind enough to lend me this dress and the necklace."

"I can't believe Ms. Khan let you borrow an expensive diamond necklace like that," Mrs. Sharma piped up, envy in her tone. "Be careful with it, *beta*."

"Oh, these are not real diamonds. They're…"

Mr. Sharma peered at her neck. "My dear girl, I would say those are one hundred percent real diamonds. And exquisite ones too. I should know. I was a jeweler's apprentice in another life."

Naina could have kissed Mr. Sharma's cheek for dropping that tidbit and pulling the team's attention away from her for a moment. Because she was sure her shock was written on her face.

Why would Zara let her borrow real diamonds? And now that she thought about it, why would she even own a dress that fit Naina's petite form when she was tall and statuesque? Why would…

She jerked her gaze to Vikram. One look at those falsely innocent eyes and the truth hit her. He had sent the dress and the diamonds to her!

A designer dress and real diamonds… What was he thinking? And why?

Anger diluted the stupid hope building in her chest. Hope was dangerous, hope made her weak.

She wanted to grab his arm and drag him through the curious spectators to demand what his game was. She wanted to tell the entire world and all the beautiful women that had made eyes at him that he was hers. She wanted to tell him, in front of this whole crowd, that she knew the real man, that she loved him for who he was beneath the mask of the Bollywood star, that she…

She loved him. So much that it stole her breath.

"Naina, what is it? You look…pale," he said, a sudden seriousness to his tone. All manner of formality was gone, all the false charm and teasing buried beneath genuine concern.

Naina heard Mrs. Sharma agree through the sudden pounding in her head.

She stared at him anew, her breath seesawing through her. Big and broad, he filled her entire vision and yet, she had no need to see or hear the rest of the world. In his beautiful eyes that saw so much and betrayed so little, in that sensual mouth that smiled far too infrequently, in the sharp nose that quivered to betray him when he wanted to remain serious with her, her entire world was in this man.

She was in love with Vikram.

A half sob, half laugh erupted from her mouth.

Scowl deepening, he took her arm and dragged her away from the avidly watching team members, his gaze not wavering from her. "I'll take you back to the resort. If you still don't feel better, we can call Dr. Mehta—"

"I'm not unwell."

"There's nothing wrong with being looked over."

His hand around her elbow, he walked her to the front of the bungalow and stuffed her into his car.

"You can't just ditch Ms. Khan." Something about the resolute set of his jaw made Naina look back. "I'm enjoying the party. I don't want to leave."

"Enough, Naina. You've already proved that you can stick it to me."

"You've made your decision, Mr. Raawal," she said, stubbornly. "You need to stop hovering around me as if you were my...keeper."

"Yes, I have made a decision."

Even without that statement, Naina got it. He had made a decision. It had been in his eyes when he'd complimented her. Because he didn't do anything without forethought. Without weighing everything.

Her pulse raced as she wondered what it was. If she could bear to be sane when she heard it.

"I don't think we should be alone right now," Naina protested, when they arrived at the resort. It felt as if the entire world had fallen quiet so that the only sound to be heard far and wide was the thudding of her heart.

His mouth flinched, his fingers tight on the steering wheel. "You sound as if you're terrified of me."

"I am." When he jerked his gaze to her, his mouth a flat line, she amended her answer. She could wound this man, she was realizing. "Not of you, exactly."

She sat like a doll while he undid her seat belt in quick movements. She went with him when he took her down the walkway to the villa they shared, straight through to her bedroom.

"Now, how about you tell me what's really wrong." His gaze ran over her face. "You still look like you're in shock."

How could she fall for a man who could control his desire and feelings as if he had access to an on/off switch? Who didn't even have an affair without calculating all the pros and cons?

She was never going to get over him, because even in this fog of fear, she knew no one would top Vikram for her. No one would know her or like her or care for her more than he did. Because he did, she knew that. Despite his own reservations. But by the same measure, would he always deny even the possibility of them being together long-term?

"I *have* received a shock," she finally mumbled.

"Did someone say something to you?"

She shook her head, one tear rolling down her cheek.

"Tell me what's bothering you."

His gentle tone made the feeling in her chest swell, until she couldn't breathe. No one had ever paid so much attention to her well-being. Not even Papa.

"Come, Dream Girl. I know I'm not a real hero but I can fix anything for you. I want to fix it for you."

"I just realized that I've fallen in love. With you." She wiped the tear from her cheek and laughed.

"With the arrogant, dominating, I-make-my-own-rules Vikram Raawal, who can't even have a fling with me because it breaks his rules."

His head jerked back, his shock clear in those beautiful eyes. "What?"

Naina fell to her bed and buried her face in her hands. "And I just told you, didn't I? Not that it makes any difference."

"You think it makes no difference to me to know that you love me?" Those simple words sounded unusual on his tongue.

"Not in the big scheme of things, no. You abhor the entire concept of love. I know you well enough for that. And by blurting it out like that, I only opened myself to your ridicule. To you pushing me away again."

He knelt in front of her and tipped her chin up. Those eyes were tender, his knuckles gentle on her cheek. As if she were precious. As if he were afraid he would mar her with his touch.

This big man, on his knees in front of her, the look in his eyes...it was an image she would never forget.

And Naina knew that while he might never love her, he did care about her. He had kept his distance not because it was easy for him but because he'd thought it was the right thing to do while she worked for him. Not because she wasn't good enough.

Because Vikram always did the right thing, did his duty. Whether it was hard, or inconvenient or even if it meant denying himself happiness.

"I would never ever ridicule you. Never. What you

have told me is a gift, Naina. Believe me, cold and calculating as I am, even I recognize it.

"Your words are a gift, Dream Girl. One I'm not sure I even deserve."

"Is it?"

"Absolutely. And even before you told me this, I had my plans for you."

"Like sneakily sending me a dress and diamonds?" She pressed her fingers to the warm stones at her throat. "Why, Vikram? I don't understand."

"I wanted you to have what you needed to go to the party."

She nodded, realizing how simple it was to him. She was now under the umbrella of protection Vikram Raawal extended. Whether she asked for it or not, he would always care about her. Give her whatever she asked. Except…himself. "You should know when I say I love you, I… I have no expectations of you. It is simply a fact. Like I love my stepmother and Maya and my neighbor's old dog Vicky."

"How charming that your neighbor's dog is named after me." He held her gaze as his own widened. "You named him, didn't you?"

She nodded and Vikram laughed. The joy in his chest was indescribable.

He had a feeling he could spend half a lifetime with her and she would still make him laugh. She'd give him more than he'd ever imagined he could take for himself. She'd already given him a future he looked forward to like he'd never done before.

And her love was a gift he would cherish. A privilege he would never take for granted. He would give her everything in return, everything he was capable of giving.

"That's the difference between you and me, Dream Girl. Because I do have expectations. Of this. Of us. A whole world of them."

She raised her face and pinned him with that stormy gaze. As if she meant to see into his very soul. As if she already could. "So you do want to be with me?"

He laughed again, to cover up the urgency he felt. Even his breathing felt shallow—his reaction to losing control of this thing between them. "Is that what you want to call it? Being with each other?" He searched for ways to say it right. "I want more than you can imagine. I want everything, Naina.

"I want you to be my wife."

The entire world seemed to have fallen silent at his admission. He couldn't even hear the waves outside beneath the dull thundering in his ears. He felt vulnerable, and he didn't like it one bit. But just this once, he promised himself. Just this once and she would give him everything in return.

"Have I rendered you mute, Dream Girl?"

She raised her gaze to his, her hands slowly coming to cradle his cheek. "Are you sure? You know you…"

"Would I offer you marriage if all I wanted was to scratch an itch?"

"No. Of course not, but…this is a…complete…"

Her swift intake of breath made him smile. Impatience fluttered through him, but he curbed it.

She turned her head, and moonlight gilded the tip of her nose, the curve of her cheek. In that moment, she was truly the most beautiful thing he had ever seen.

He pushed himself to his feet, settled down next to her and pulled her to him. She let him arrange her to his satisfaction, her curvy body settling against him with a sensual slide that made his heartbeat jump. Her palms landed against his chest, her face half hidden in the curve of his neck.

"Talk to me, Naina. Tell me what you're thinking. Don't ever take away your words," he said, burying his nose in her hair. She smelled like coconuts and lemon and something so incredibly luscious that desire began a beat in his veins. Just the graze of her body, the scent of her skin was enough to drown him in memories of their time together.

Of the incredible pleasure he'd found with her. Of the utter feeling of peace he'd felt holding her in his arms.

Small fingers rubbed at his chest, the weight of her voluptuous breasts against his ribs incredibly arousing. "You can have anyone, any woman in the world. And I'm just..." She laughed and it was the sweetest sound he'd ever heard. "I mean, not that I'm not great. I'm just not particularly beautiful or brave or ambitious or smart or fierce or..."

"Watch out what you say about my girl," he said, hearing the thread of ache buried deep in those words. It wasn't exactly insecurity. It was a question that had never been answered by people who should have, a question that gained more and more control over one's life the longer it went unaddressed.

"I'm so...ordinary, Vikram. Very much so. Nothing..."

"I'd like to point out that everything you've said is wrong."

"How?" she said, the word so full of hope that he had to consider his words carefully.

"Firstly, the idea that I could have any woman I wanted is such ridiculous thinking. I'm really disappointed you haven't already deconstructed such an arbitrary, archaic thought, as if women were meant to be simply...had." She giggled and pinched him and Vikram felt as if the entire world was in his arms right then. "Secondly, if I've learned one thing in life—and since I'm more than a decade older than you, you have to admit that I've seen and heard and done more things in my life than you have—"

"Oh, God, I can see you're going to use this to dominate every argument we will have..." she muttered into his chest, her mouth a warm, open pocket against his throat.

"It is in the ordinary that life and magic happen. Thirdly, all that is completely moot because I don't want anyone else. I want you, Dream Girl. Only you."

He could feel her softening against his words, against his touch. Against him. He nuzzled his nose into her face.

"But, Vikram..."

"Shh… Dream Girl," he said, pressing his mouth to the corner of hers. That quieted her immediately. "Do you believe that if I give you my word, I'd never ever break it?"

"Absolutely. From the first moment."

"Good. Now believe me when I say you've given me a future that I never allowed myself to even imagine I could have."

He opened his mouth and whispered against the silky soft skin of her jaw, loving the taste of her on his tongue. "So think of this. Take your time. I trust you, too, Naina. I trust that once you make a commitment to me, you will keep it. And I have never trusted anyone like that ever before."

Slowly, against his body's every wish, he untangled her from him. Or him from her. And stood up.

She frowned. "You're leaving?"

She looked so forlorn that he took her hand in his and pressed his mouth to the soft skin at her wrist. Her pulse moved through him like a song, sending his heart into overdrive. "You have a lot to think on. I…don't want to persuade you in any way. And if I stay, I will." He cursed and she looked at him with those wide eyes. "I will use the hunger I see in your eyes to persuade you to do anything.

"And I don't want to. So even as it kills me, I'm going to walk away, Dream Girl. Come to me when you're ready.

"Come to me, be my wife and I'll lay the entire world at your feet."

CHAPTER ELEVEN

Naina twisted the knob on the door and went in without knocking. It hadn't been more than a few hours. She hadn't gotten a wink of sleep and she knew she wasn't going to.

When she'd seen dawn paint the sky a brilliant pink, she'd given up and gotten out of bed. It wasn't as if she had to think and decide. She wasn't like him. She already knew her heart. She knew that while he would never say the words she longed to hear, this was enough for her. What he could give was more than enough.

He wasn't sleeping either. He was sitting upright on a huge bed in the center of the room holding the latest version of the script, bifocal glasses perched on his face, looking utterly cute. Bare shoulders and lightly haired chest on display made her swallow.

She stood like that, with her back pressed to the hard wood, her hands folded at her midriff. Suddenly, she felt strangely shy. For all that they'd been so intimate with each other at the ball, it had been in the dark of the night. In a way, it had even been easier. Easier to shed her inhibitions, easier to live in that moment, because at the end of it, she'd known she was going home alone. There had only been pleasure.

This intimacy, however, was different. This had vulnerability and awkwardness and tenderness and the slow burn of desire. Of anticipation.

When his gaze swept over her from her hair, into which she'd slathered that awful conditioning oil, to her bare feet, she realized she still had on her old oversized T-shirt and she'd taken her bra off as always. Thank God she'd at least washed her face and was blessed with good skin.

He put away the script and took off his glasses. Pushing up on the bed, he folded his arms behind his head and gave her the once-over again. The sheet slipped downward to reveal the happy trail on his abdomen and the waistband of his pajamas.

God, she could just lick him up when he looked like that.

"Are you planning to stay by the door all night?"

"I barged in to tell you my decision."

"And?"

"I realized belatedly that maybe I should have dressed up for the occasion."

"Dressed up?"

"Not formally, I mean. Just worn something silky and not applied this oil thing to my hair."

His mouth twitched. "Do you own silky somethings?"

"Not really."

"Is that oil thing so repellent?"

"Of course not. It doesn't have any scent at all.

Don't you dare laugh at me, Vikram. My curls go haywire if I don't tame them at night."

"I wouldn't dare laugh at you, Naina." He sighed. And that broad, hard chest flexed impressively. "You…every time I think I know you, you surprise me some more. You make me laugh, Dream Girl. Now how about you tell me what's going on in that head?"

"I'm saying yes. To your proposal. I want to be your wife. I couldn't sleep and I really wanted to come in here and tell you. And now, now I feel like I should've worn something sexier or put makeup on or just…you know, done something to mark the occasion as special."

"You make everything special, Naina. Haven't you got that yet?"

Naina shook her head. She knew she was being stubborn, but she couldn't help it. "It's not every day an ordinary girl gets proposed to, is it? You're the stuff of dreams, Vikram. I have this…crazy, over-whelming urge to make this night different for you. When you're a crotchety ninety-year-old man, I want you to think back on this night and go…yippee!"

A wicked light shone in his eyes. "So what I'm getting is that you really want to wow me?"

She nodded.

"Take that T-shirt off, then. Only if you're com-fortable, that is. You always have to tell me what is okay and what is not, Naina."

Vikram had barely finished his sentence before she caught the hem of the tee and pulled it up over her head. The movement loosened the clip in her hair and even in their tamed state, her curls framed her face.

His breath slammed into Vikram's throat as he greedily studied this woman who was going to bring him to his knees very soon. He wanted to be on his knees right now, pressing his face into her cute belly button and even lower. He wanted to fill his every breath with the scent of her arousal.

Her skin was smooth and silky. Her breasts full and high, her waist tiny. White cotton panties made her brown skin gleam. She lifted both her arms to pull her hair back and that pushed up her breasts even more. His erection pressed upward, his breath shallow.

"I think I know what would make tonight special for you," she said, while he drank in her stunning curvy body.

"What?" he said, his voice hoarse.

"That night at the ball, you gave me a fantasy evening. I want to return the favor. I…want this time to be all about you."

Vikram pushed away the soft duvet and straightened up some more. "My pleasure is in you finding yours, Naina."

"No, Vikram." She pouted and he wanted to sink his teeth into that lip. "Don't be a gentleman. Don't treat me with kid gloves, please. This is as much about me as it is about you. How do you like it best?"

He saw it then—her vulnerability when it came to him. Because she thought herself not particularly beautiful compared to the women of his circle. God, if only he could make her see how he saw her, right then. How gloriously fierce and sexy she looked.

Since he couldn't, he decided to give her what she was asking for. To show her how much he wanted her.

"Fast and hard," he whispered without a beat. "But not without you climaxing first."

She nodded seriously, as if he was giving her life-saving instructions. "So what should I do first?"

"Are you wet for me, Dream Girl?"

Pink streaked her cheeks and the Neanderthal in him loved that only he saw her like this. But she didn't let her obvious shyness stop her. Slowly, she sank her fingers under the cotton of her panties, her brow furrowed in concentration.

"Oh…" she whispered and it went straight to his shaft. Hell, forget fast and hard, he was going to embarrass himself at this rate. "I'm very wet," she said with a languorous smile.

He patted the place next to him. And she came. Once she lay down on the bed, he pushed her thighs wide and rolled to lie between them. He sank one hand into her hair and pulled up her face and took her mouth in a blisteringly hungry kiss. True to her word, she gave as good as she got.

She thrust her tongue into his mouth and licked him, her soft groans falling on his skin like sizzling raindrops. He pulled away, and leaned his forehead against hers. "Naina, this is definitely what you want?"

Clear brown eyes looked into his, and he wondered if she could really see into his soul. God, this woman made him hard with just one look. And she understood what he was asking too.

That this wasn't just about tonight. This was about their entire lives together, enmeshed. This was a commitment he would never break. And he needed to know she knew that.

She clasped his cheek and yet the tenderness didn't break the heat of the moment. "I want to marry you, Vikram. I want to spend the rest of my life with you. I'm going to be your hot, only seventy-eight-year-old wife when you're that crotchety ninety-year-old."

And then he didn't wait. He gave them both what they wanted.

He pushed off his pajamas and thrust into her wet heat in one deep stroke that sent her spine arching toward him like a bolt of lightning.

He let her get used to him for a few seconds and stayed still, while busying his mouth with the elegant line of her neck, the thrust of her breasts. He licked her nipple before drawing it deep into his mouth. Her hands in his hair told her how much she liked it.

With increasingly loud moans, she goaded him on. He pulled out and thrust back in and she groaned again.

He brought her hand to where they were joined. Eyes wide, she looked down and then back up at him. "Touch yourself. Tell me when you're close."

She nodded, and Vikram filled his hands with her buttocks and dragged her even closer. Tilting her hips just a little, he pistoned in and out of her, desire a clamoring shout in his veins now. And she never looked away from him.

Finally, when she threw her head back and clenched against him in ecstasy, he let the last thread of his control fracture.

Naina woke up when she felt a hard arm around her waist, constricting her movements.

"A stampeding elephant moves less than you when you sleep," a voice whispered at her ear and she smiled.

Slowly, she turned, and there he was, lying on his side, looking down at her.

A burst of joy filled her chest. "Maybe we can sleep in different bedrooms like the maharajas and maharanis of the past. You can come visit me whenever you're in the mood."

He scowled. She giggled and tapped his brow.

He caught her finger and tugged it into his mouth. He licked the pad and sucked on her finger and Naina wiggled under the sheet covering them. She sent her hands on a quest and found warm, rough velvety skin. She stroked him to her heart's content—the silky hair, the taut nipples, the slab of his abdominal muscles, and further down...

He caught her wrist, and stilled her. He turned her until her back was to him and cradled her face in his hand. At her bottom, he was rock-hard. She gasped in a breath, ready again. Ready for whatever he wanted.

With his thigh tucked between hers, the pressure at her core was delicious. His fingers played with her nipple, sending arrows of want deep down.

"That's not the kind of marriage I want," he whispered, licking the rim of her ear.

"No?"

He bit the soft shell. "Remember when you said you were called old-fashioned and that it was an arbitrary construct forcibly put on women?"

"I can't believe you remember all my lectures."

"Every word, Dream Girl. But I have no problem admitting that I am terribly old-fashioned. I want the world and its myriad, talented artists and set designers to know you're mine. I believe in claiming what's mine."

She turned around in his arms. "I...we don't have to rush into this, do we?"

"That's a relative term. We don't have to get married tomorrow, as much as I want to. Daadi will never forgive me. Say at the end of next month, when she's home from London?"

"I just need time to..."

"Decide?"

"No. To...take this all in."

When he scowled, she went for his mouth. Softly. Slowly. In a sensuous whisper. Almost a supplication. She rubbed her mouth against his, and stilled. And he understood the stillness. That first slide of their lips breathed through him, memories of that first evening only amplifying the sensation now.

Her tongue tentatively licking at his lower lip, pleading for entry rather than barging in. And when he did, with a harsh exhale, the tip of her tongue swirled against his, and then retreated. And then she did it all over again.

In and out, tease and taunt, lick here and a nip there, she wrung slow, soft pleasure out of him until he was panting. But he let her. He let her take whatever she wanted, however she wanted him. He let her explore and seek and retreat and revel in the simple kiss.

"You're all I want, Vikram," Naina whispered against his swollen lips. "It's not even like I want a big wedding. As long as Jaya Ma and Maya can make it, I'm okay with anything."

"Good," he whispered, the scowl disappearing.

Naina turned around again and nudged at the hardness with her bum. "Now will you just show me how it's possible this way?"

He laughed against her back and it was like a symphony playing over her skin. He lifted her leg and pushed in slowly from behind and Naina thought she might die from the onslaught of pleasure.

"Let me guess," she said, her breath seesawing through her, with his every firm thrust. "This is your favorite position."

His hand sneaked down from between her breasts, over her belly to unerringly land on her nub. He flicked it and she felt fire rain down her belly. "How do you know?" he asked, working her with a practiced ease that she was so incredibly grateful for.

"You have all the control like this."

He dug his teeth into her shoulder, counteracting the rivulets of pleasure pooling down at her sex. "True, Dream Girl. But I would never cheat you out of your pleasure."

As his thrusts became faster, he turned her face and kissed her and Naina knew, as she climaxed more fiercely than ever before, that he would always keep his word.

CHAPTER TWELVE

"I THINK THE script is brilliant. You've outdone yourself, bhai," Virat said over the video call, his fingers still shuffling the pages on the desk in front of him and making notes.

Vikram smiled, feeling more than a sliver of satisfaction at hearing the awe in his brother's words. It wasn't that he didn't trust his own intuition. But he had spent most of his career making movies for commercial success and he'd begun to doubt his vision. He'd started this concept as an homage to his grandfather but it had become his own soul project.

Today instead of feeling the sensation of having shackles around him whenever he contemplated a new project, Vikram felt a simple joy. Saving his parents from definite ruin had cost him a lot of his artistic integrity. And yet for Virat and Anya and even his parents' sake, Vikram knew he would make the same choices all over again.

"And yet you continue to slash it with that awful red pen of yours."

Virat looked up and frowned slightly. "Okay, so

don't rain down fury on me. But there's just one element missing. And no, I still can't figure out what it is. Just give me another week to sit on this, yeah?"

Vikram nodded, even as he remembered that Naina had said she knew what was missing. She didn't know a lot about making movies and yet, he trusted her intuition when it came to people. She was also one of the few people who would give him her honest opinion, who challenged him to look past his own blind spots.

Look at how easily she'd woven herself into the fabric of his own life.

In just nine days, he'd already gotten used to waking up with her curled up against him. It was disconcerting to say the least that after thirty-six years, someone could become so addictive in the matter of a few days. But he had no other word that would fit what was happening.

Marriage had seemed like something that would only work for him with someone like Zara, who would never ask him for more than he'd give. And Naina didn't either. And yet, he often woke up in the middle of the night to realize she had a way of taking what he wasn't even sure he could give.

There was a magical, addictive quality to their union that did...give him pause. Once she was his wife, that strangeness would become normal, he reassured himself. Naina was so far away from any life partner he'd imagined in his wildest dreams that the novelty of it was bound to go to his head.

"I'm surprised you're still in the Maldives when everyone else has flown home."

Vikram shrugged. "Aren't you the one who's always saying I need to relax more? Go with the flow?"

"But it's not just the island paradise that's wrought this difference. You're smiling and you didn't even yell at me when I said I needed time to sit with the script and make changes to it. Even Anya said you sounded different on your call with her."

"I trust your judgment, Virat. I know I have made you doubt that before, both professionally and personally, and I apologize for it."

Virat blew out a breath. "I guess we're doing this then. Then I apologize for attacking you like I did last time. I'm not unaware, nor is Anya, of how much you've given us at great personal cost to yourself, *bhai*.

"It's not a debt I can ever repay."

Vikram swallowed the lump in his throat. He simply nodded, glad that they had sorted their differences. Oh, they would absolutely butt heads again—they were far too different in their temperaments not to, but things would be okay between them.

"Come, *bhai*, spill it," Virat prompted again.

"I'm engaged," Vikram said simply.

A stillness came over his brother's features, all the more disturbing since Virat had always been a ball of fiery energy from childhood. Every school had thrown him out, every teacher raised their hands when it had come to him. Even as an adult, there was a sense of constant motion, an excessive energy about his brother that Vikram always found disconcerting. And yet now…it was as if he'd pulled a shroud over himself, masking the real him.

But Vikram knew his brother well. Very well. They were comrades who'd lived through the war zone that had been their parents' marriage.

Virat wasn't simply angry at his announcement. It was something else. Something Vikram wasn't sure even his brother understood.

"You said proposing to Zara had been an impulse. A mistake. You said you'd been relieved when she turned you down. God, *bhai*, don't tell me she's accepted you after all. You're not right for each other."

He knew he was being a beast but Vikram wanted confirmation of the sudden doubt niggling at him. "Are you so sure about that, Virat?"

His brother pushed a shaking hand through his hair suddenly looking sick to his stomach, and Vikram realized he'd gone too far. That whatever was between Zara and Virat was no joking matter. "It's Naina," he said, eager now to remove that devastated look from Virat's eyes. "Not Zara. Like I said, that was just a momentary madness."

Virat's jaw dropped. "Naina as in Ms. Menon who shattered your ego, the Naina that you hired to be your temporary PA?"

Vikram laughed. "Yes. That Naina."

Virat leaned into the camera, as if to get a better look at Vikram. "*Bhai*…you're serious?"

Vikram simply nodded. "We haven't made it public yet. So keep it to yourself."

"She's not your type."

"I was unaware I had a type," he said flatly.

"She's innocent and full of heart, and one of a kind."

Vikram didn't like the admiration in Virat's voice. Even though he knew his brother was teasing him now. And that every word was true. "She's also undemanding, low maintenance and yes, she's honest about what she feels for me and she's never going to break my trust."

"You're marrying the poor woman because she's low maintenance?" His brother sounded appalled.

"I'm marrying her because she doesn't play games like everyone else in our industry, Virat. Naina knows my shortcomings, knows exactly what I can and can't give her and yet, she's all in. After all the drama of Papa and Mama's marriage, this is exactly the kind of—"

"Bhai..."

Vikram didn't need the warning from Virat. His skin prickled. He hung up the call and turned around to find Naina standing at the entrance to the room.

Her eyes looked even wider than usual, the acute hurt in them pinning him to the spot.

"You wanted to marry Zara?"

He hated feeling defensive and yet she made him feel it. "It was just a crazy, impulsive thing. I didn't really mean it."

"But you don't do crazy impulsive things. You weigh your every word and action. So...what happened?"

"We don't need a postmortem of it, Naina."

"You proposed to your best friend. It had to have meant something. Even for you."

"Even for me?"

"Yes, you."

"I had a rough year. Call it a midlife crisis. I asked her one evening and she laughed it off and that was that. Really, Naina, you're making too much of this."

"Oh, yeah, I forgot. I'm supposed to be undemanding. Low maintenance. I'm supposed to give you all my trust and come running when you whistle, so that you can throw me a treat and then walk away when you're done. I'm not supposed to create drama. That last one is my most attractive quality to you, isn't it?"

Vikram rubbed his hand over his face and cursed. He hadn't meant for it to sound like a dismissal. Or a cruelly neat summary of what role she filled in his life. It had been a glib, defensive thing to say to Virat. Because how could he explain to his brother what he felt for her when he didn't understand it himself? When he didn't really trust it? When the fear of one day losing her kept him up at night?

"I will apologize if the way I said it hurt you. But it's not far from the truth, Naina. What we have is—"

"Am I just a replacement for Zara since she turned you down? Because I have to tell you, you're getting a bad bargain, Vikram."

Vikram could feel himself shaking, losing control of this. "You're insulting not just yourself with that ridiculous comparison, but me too. And the commitment we've made to each other."

She met his gaze and nodded but he saw that they weren't done. He could see the same fears he felt in her eyes. "You're right. I know that you and Zara are best friends. I know that and yet..." Confusion and something like grief suffused her features. "Please tell me this was before you met me at the ball. Before we slept with each other."

"If it's just to keep your timeline straight, yes, it was before I met you. Before you came into my life. Before you—"

"So why hide it from me then?"

"I didn't hide it as much as I decided it was irrelevant to us. I still stand by that decision."

"And that should be enough for me?" she said, tilting her chin in challenge.

"Yes."

She sat down and pushed the tangled mass of her hair away from her face. "I thought you were one person who would never hurt me. I didn't even care that you..."

"That I what?" Vikram felt like he was standing on the edge of a cliff, blindfolded, completely unaware of how deep the gorge below was.

"That you didn't love me back. I was okay with it, honestly. I know you're not given to sweet words and sugary declarations but your actions said enough for me. I was more than happy with the fact that you wanted me in your life forever. That you..."

"I still do," he said, a shaft of fear cracking through the shell he kept around himself.

The power this woman could wield over him sent him into a cold sweat. And fear was something he'd always hated. Despised. It made his words curt. "So the question to ask is have *you* changed your mind?"

And she responded to that harshness, her mouth flinching. Her eyes widening further. Her fingers in her lap tangled and untangled. "No, yes. I don't know. All I know is that I need to rethink this. I need to—"

"Rethink what? God, Naina, look at me and say whatever the hell is going on in that head of yours."

"I don't know if I can marry you." She spat the words out and he could see the anger in her now. But it didn't touch him. Couldn't touch him.

If it did, he would be lost. And despite everything life had thrown at him, he had never allowed anything to make him into that lost creature that depended on someone else for its emotional well-being, like his father had his mother. "Either it's a yes or a no."

Naina saw the instant the shutter fell down over his features. As if it was simply a matter of pulling down a curtain. She suddenly wished she'd gone into his arms. When he touched her, when he held her, it felt like nothing and no one could hurt her. Like nothing could ever come between them.

"I love you, Vikram. So much. That's what makes this complicated."

"You have a funny way of showing you love me, Dream Girl. Just like the entire world."

"You're right. That you proposed to Zara in a crazy moment doesn't change anything. Maybe you hid it from me because it's such an uncharacteristic thing for you to have done. Because you hate weaknesses, don't you? You'd hate for anybody to think you needed someone in your life. But I do understand one thing now."

"And what is that?"

"That this marriage would mean completely different things to us both. For me, it meant entering into a holy bond with a man I love, and trust. A man who'd give me his highest commitment.

"But for you, it's a way of locking me down. A way of having what you want without the messy tangle of emotions to impede you. A way of giving me everything, the entire world, without actually giving me the one thing you should give.

"You're a businessman in this too, Vikram, as you are in everything you do. I'm a no-risk investment. That's why this is easy for you.

"I was awed by the fact that not only did you want to be with me but that you wanted to spend your whole life with me. I thought that was the ultimate commitment. For all the clever words you give me, I'm never going to be your equal in our marriage because you'll always hold part of yourself back. Because you have nothing to lose by marrying me and everything to gain.

"I deserve more than that. So I need time and distance from you to properly think this over. I need to—"

"Distance and time are not going to change a thing. I had years to become what I am today, Naina. This is another foolish demand of so-called romantic love…this expectation that people will change for you, that suddenly they can grow new personalities, that one morning, I'll wake up and absolutely believe in love…is downright ridiculous. You're giving up what's real, what's here, for some fantasy version of life that's not true."

She nodded then. "You truly think this is only about three little words? Or about asking you to change for me?"

"Then what the hell is it that you want from me?"

"Nothing. I do love you. I'll always love you because you made me love myself, Vikram. You gave me myself back. No one else did that for me. And if I agree to marry you knowing what I do now, if I continue this pattern of loving you so much, worried that I might lose you at some point because you don't feel the same, then I'm right back where I started. Do you see?

"This is me doing what you're always urging me to do—protecting myself from hurt. From people who would use my love and affection to achieve what they want, what's best for them.

"See, what you've been preaching to me all along has finally sunk in. I'm doing what's best for me."

She turned away from him, every inch of her trembling. Every cell in her hoping that he would swallow the distance between them and take her into his arms. But also just as terrified that if he did, she wouldn't be able to help herself from going back to him.

In her misery, it took her a few minutes to hear the silence behind her. She'd thought it would hurt less if she was the one who walked away first. Instead of being the one who was always left behind.

Her limbs shaking, Naina realized it made no difference at all. It still hurt like hell.

CHAPTER THIRTEEN

VIKRAM PUSHED HIS hand into his shaving kit looking for the card he'd stuck in there. He usually immediately saved an important contact on his phone but then, he wasn't his normal self anymore.

Something sharp pricked his finger and he pulled back with a filthy curse. A drop of blood welled up on his skin. He pressed a cotton ball against it and upended the leather shaving bag onto the black marble countertop.

A black metal dangly earring with tiny fake pearls shining around the base winked at him.

"I got this one at a street bazar in Hyderabad when I lived there one summer."

He picked up the *jhumka* and smiled. God, he couldn't believe he remembered every detail of her bargaining with some bloke in her funny dialect of Hindi. Naina had told him the story behind every pair of earrings one night when he'd complained about her things being everywhere.

Colorful scarves on different drafts of the script. Tubes of lipstick—always some gorgeous shade of red—seemed to multiply and take over among his clothes. She'd completely taken over his bedroom and he knew now, his heart.

He'd threatened to throw them all away if one more earring stuck into his backside at night and she'd been truly horrified. When he'd arrogantly reassured her that she'd have her pick of rare gems and jewelry to replace these ones, she'd been close to tears. So he had kissed her, promising to never throw anything of hers away.

"I know it's hard for you to understand, Vikram. But I don't want anything from you. Do you get that?"

He'd shaken his head. Because he didn't. Because he wanted to shower her with everything money could buy. He wanted her to live in the lap of luxury and never worry about another loan payment. But every time the matter of finances came up, she'd shut him down.

"The whole world is going to say I've landed myself a nice upgraded lifestyle. But your standing in the world, your various mansions, your cars, even your star power...they are all just window dressing, Vikram. The real you that only I get to see, the man beneath the megastar...that's my prize. You're my true prize."

He'd said nothing in return to her. On guard, constantly wondering what she'd demand if he said those things. He'd shown her instead with his kisses and his mouth and his fingers, driving her higher and higher and higher and then holding her tightly when she fell. She'd told him again and again, making herself vulnerable to him even while he continued to protect himself.

"I'm a no-risk investment," she'd said on that last day, and he realized now how right she had been. *"For all the clever words you give me, I'll never be your equal in our marriage, because you'll always hold part of yourself back."*

No, she was wrong about that. Those were only the lies he'd told himself.

Even when he hadn't recognized it, he'd been falling for Naina. God, he'd fallen for her so hard that very first time when she'd torn into him. When she'd told him so clearly what she thought he could be if he tried to change.

He just hadn't accepted it.

Two weeks since she'd walked out on him and yet she'd already left her mark on him. Already changed him in ways he was only realizing now.

Take for example the call he had received yesterday from his parents. They were going to celebrate their fortieth wedding anniversary in a fortnight's time with a huge bash, he'd been informed, and would Vikram please approve the budget and the event planner they were planning to hire and release the funds.

So he wished both his parents all the fun planning the party in such a polite note, released the funds and hung up the call without any questions, or demands or ultimatums.

His mother had called him back within minutes, inquiring if he was unwell.

He laughed now, wondering why he hadn't seen it this way before. He had built enough of a fortune that his parents could throw a bash or two and not make a dent in it. As for how they'd conduct themselves in front of the media and the others in the industry, nothing he said or did was going to change them now. When they hadn't all his life.

People that were important to him knew of him from his own reputation, his work ethic, his word. Nothing they did or said was going to change the path of his life. Not anymore now, and not for the past fifteen years.

It was as if a tremendous weight had been lifted off his shoulders. As if some invisible chains that had been binding him had suddenly been yanked off and he was free now.

Free to move forward.

Free to live his own life.

Free to pursue his own future with the woman he loved with all his heart.

The party was in full swing by the time Naina walked through the lavishly decorated foyer. She rubbed her hand down the pale pink sleeveless blouse she'd worn over another long cotton white skirt embroidered with beautiful yellow flowers. Jaya Ma and Maya had been horrified when she'd defiantly refused to dress up for an evening hobnobbing with the royalty of Bollywood.

This was the second party she was walking into at a Raawal residence. But this time, she was here as herself. Just Naina. Simply Naina.

The Naina who took risks.

The Naina who liked helping people.

The Naina who sometimes loved too much.

She wasn't here to impress anyone or to make herself feel better or to catch anyone's eye. She was here for herself. To make connections. To build a career at her own, slow pace. To live her life to the fullest.

When Virat had called her and insisted that she attend the anniversary party of his parents, she'd instantly agreed. Caught him by surprise. Because, of course, he knew his brother and she had been together. And that they had fallen apart just as spectacularly.

Virat wasn't inviting her as a favor or because he felt sorry for her. He was inviting her because she was part of the team now. She was officially part of Raawal House's Magnum Opus. And now she was working for Zara Khan, who'd been given the role in the film that Vikram had intended, she was going to see Vikram on the sets of the biopic anyway. Better to get used to seeing him. Of longing for him. Of wishing things had been different.

Because as much as the anger and hurt had slowly fallen away, the love she felt for him had stayed. And she'd made her peace with it.

In the meantime, she was going to stay right there and maximize her career opportunities. And try to help her stepmother a little with her own career, if she could. It wasn't as if Jaya Ma was not talented. She, like Naina herself, simply needed more opportunities, more exposure.

"You okay, *beta*?" her stepmother whispered in her ear and Naina nodded.

They circulated through the main lounge and the back garden and then lined up to greet the family. The bouquet of flowers she'd brought as a gift felt extra heavy in her damp hands as Naina craned her head to look at the family members greeting the guests. Neither Virat nor Vikram were present. But Daadiji was, newly arrived from London.

Naina swallowed when Vikram's mother's gaze, then her husband's, suddenly fell on her. Then Daadiji waved at her with a broad smile. One by one, it seemed as if all the crowd were craning their heads to look at her. Strangers, acquaintances, there was no one who wasn't staring in her direction, mouths agog, expressions full of awe.

A sudden silence fell over the crowd as if someone had sent a signal. For a hysterical second, Naina wondered if she was in a nightmare. Was she naked? Had she walked in with her face pack still on?

She freed one hand and tried to reach for her stepmother. Her arm met empty air. Even Jaya Ma had ditched her. She swallowed and looked up at the beautiful crystal chandelier on the high ceiling and she saw Zara standing on the upper balcony, with Virat by her side. Zara looked as though she had tears in her eyes and Virat…he gave Naina an encouraging nod.

And then into the silence came that old Tamil song. Her mother's favorite. Her own eyes now full of tears, she simply stood there, letting the song seep into her. Letting it wash away all the sadness in her heart and filling it with fresh, bursting hope.

Because she knew then. She knew why they were all looking at her. Knew why her soul felt as if it had been slammed with an awareness she couldn't deny.

Heart in her throat, Naina turned. Empty space greeted her until she looked down.

He was there—her very own hero. On his knees. In front of the entire world. Because Naina had no doubt this would be all over the internet in a few minutes.

Vikram Raawal on his knees for a very ordinary girl. Vikram Raawal in love. The Vikram Raawal who'd always walked the line of propriety with iron-clad rules.

Her breath slammed into her with such force that Naina thought she might just melt into a puddle.

In a half white kurta with gold piping at the Nehru collar, with his unruly hair pushed away to reveal those aristocratic features, he was broad and big and so gorgeous and…

And in his hands was a small velvet box with a ring that looked like a family heirloom that could probably be dated back a thousand years. A small oval ruby nestled amidst tiny diamonds…

Tears fell over her cheeks making the diamonds flicker extra hard. She shook her head, hating that she was making a mess of her face.

"Won't you look at me, Dream Girl?"

There was no charm, no mockery, only tenderness in his voice. Nothing but unadulterated emotion. Such need that it made his voice hoarse.

And she finally met his gaze. "I... I never said you had to do this. I never demanded that you prove anything to me. Never."

"Ahh...but I promised myself I'd always give you more than you ask, Naina. I never want you to doubt me again. Never doubt that you and only you have everything of me. Everything, including my heart.

"This is the ring that Daadu gave Daadi. I asked her for it because I thought I needed all the luck I can get and she gave it to us with all her blessings. But if you don't like it—"

"I love it," she whispered, because she did.

He looked at her with such naked adoration in his eyes that Naina swallowed. "I'm all in, Dream Girl.

"You could walk away from here without another backward look and I would still love you. They could all laugh at the cliché I've become and I would still love you. Twenty years later, I could be the worst-case scenario for every Romeo out there...stories and songs could be written about me—horrible rap songs, and Virat will probably make a movie about all this, just to get back at me and I would still absolutely love you."

And then Naina was laughing and crying, because God, she loved this man so much.

"Whether you say yes or not, I will love you from

now to forever, Naina. Forgive this old guy for not being wise enough to see it sooner."

"Stop it," she said, smacking him on the shoulder. "You're not old. And you're just imperfectly perfect."

"Virat told me that you were the one who tweaked the film's storyline in the end."

"I...the more I read it, the more I realized it had no true happy ending." She pressed her hand to his mouth. "I know you want to make this a serious movie but who said historical sagas that show the Independence Movement shouldn't also have a little happiness too, Vikram? It doesn't have to have such a bleak landscape to be taken seriously.

"I know your grandfather didn't actually meet and fall in love with your grandmother until later on. But why can't you tweak the timing in the film a little and give them both the happy-ever-after they deserve?"

He laughed and shook his head. "I think that ending makes it shine, Dream Girl. I just wondered why you didn't come and tell me?"

"Because I didn't want to take anything away from what you've already achieved, Vikram. And I never want you to think I'm in this for the opportunities you could give me."

"I never thought that, Dream Girl. Ever."

"I knew Virat would give me an objective opinion of my idea. And Zara's already arranged for me to talk to another producer about another script idea I have. I can't tell you how excited I am. And it's all thanks to you."

"I didn't do anything," he said.

"You set me on this path. You gave me the initial push and the confidence."

"You're the one who's saving me," he said "From myself. From a world that sometimes only takes and doesn't give back. From a life that was nothing but an endless cycle of loneliness and broken promises.

"You're my always and forever. My new beginning and my happy-ever-after. My very own love story. Will you marry me, Naina?

"Because my life is nothing but a cheap, commercial sellout without you by my side, Dream Girl."

She went close to him and he buried his face in her belly. She dropped the bouquet and buried her fingers in his hair thinking her heart might just explode with all the happiness filling it. "Yes, I will marry you, Vikram. And for the rest of my life, I will love you. I will never doubt you. And I..." Her knees did finally give in.

And he caught her, her real hero.

Naina fell into his arms, his mouth claiming hers with a need that quivered through her entire body. Applause broke out around them. She heard Daadiji and Zara and Virat cheering and Jaya Ma screaming, "That's my stepdaughter. That's my girl," at the top of her voice.

She laughed into his kiss and he bit her gently and then he was putting the ring on her finger and Naina was terrified that it might all be just a dream. She laughed a lot, they both touched Daadiji's feet,

Virat squeezed her into a bone-cracking hug and Zara kissed her cheek and hugged Vikram.

His mother, even more beautiful up close, kept snatching looks at her son as he looked at Naina. Waiting to be introduced. Naina felt a flicker of shame lick up her cheeks. God, this had been their anniversary party and Vikram had just simply hijacked it.

She walked up to Mrs. Raawal and introduced herself, knowing Vikram wouldn't be able to avoid his mother after that. His arm came around her waist not two seconds later.

"I'm sorry for...interrupting your party, Mrs. Raawal. I'm..."

"Oh, please. I didn't mind at all. In fact, whatever the reason my son wanted to prove to you that he loves you, I'm glad for it. I got to see up close just how much he adores you." She offered her cheek and Naina dutifully kissed it. "And please call me Vandana."

"Will you bring her to meet us properly after the party?" she asked her son, a wealth of hope in her eyes. "I would like to get to know this girl who's made my son so happy."

Naina squeezed Vikram's hand for all she was worth when she saw the instant refusal on his lips. He pressed a kiss to her temple and smiled. His expression and his words when he turned to her were tempered. And Naina had never been so proud of this man she loved. "Not just yet, but soon, Mama. I want her to myself for a little while."

Mrs. Raawal nodded and kissed Naina's cheek. "Welcome to the family, Naina. I have no words to tell you how glad we are that you're in his life."

Naina swallowed at the open ache in her eyes. They left in a whirlwind of camera flashes from a myriad of mobile phones. But instead of driving across the city to his own home, they stopped at Zara's flat for the night. Which was much closer.

Once they entered Zara's expansive flat, Naina turned to him. "I'm… I have no words. I know you hate that kind of drama and invasion into your private life… I never needed it, Vikram. I just wanted your love." She pressed her hand and her mouth to his chest, loving the tight squeeze of his arms around her.

"I know you didn't ask for it. But you deserve it, Dream Girl. You're the best thing that walked into my life and I will constantly try to let everyone know, including you, how much I love you, and you'll just have to put up with that."

"I love you too," Naina whispered, knowing that she finally had her very own hero.

* * * * *

Head over heels for
Claiming His Bollywood Cinderella?
You'll love the next instalment in the
Born into Bollywood miniseries
coming soon!

And why not explore these other
Tara Pammi stories?

Sicilian's Bride for a Price
An Innocent to Tame the Italian
A Deal to Carry the Italian's Heir
The Flaw in His Marriage Plan

All available now

WE HOPE YOU ENJOYED
THIS BOOK FROM

 HARLEQUIN
PRESENTS

Escape to exotic locations where passion knows no bounds.

Welcome to the glamorous lives of royals and billionaires, where passion knows no bounds. Be swept into a world of luxury, wealth and exotic locations.

8 NEW BOOKS AVAILABLE EVERY MONTH!

#3869 THE QUEEN'S IMPOSSIBLE BOSS
The Christmas Princess Swap
by Natalie Anderson

Switching places with her twin was supposed to give Queen Jade two weeks free from duty. Not ignite an instant desire for her sister's billionaire boss! Yet perhaps Jade and Alvaro Byrne can explore their unrivaled connection...just for Christmas!

#3870 STOLEN TO WEAR HIS CROWN
The Queen's Guard
by Marcella Bell

Scientist Mina has finally secured her dream job when she's stolen from the interview room! She's taken directly to the palace chapel, where the terms of a secret betrothal mean marrying powerful King Zayn—immediately!

#3871 THE ITALIAN'S FINAL REDEMPTION
by Jackie Ashenden

Vincenzo de Santi has dedicated his life to redeeming his family's crimes. So when Lucy Armstrong offers evidence about her nefarious father in exchange for her freedom, he'll show no mercy. No matter how innocent—or tempting—she seems...

#3872 BOUND AS HIS BUSINESS-DEAL BRIDE
by Kali Anthony

To save her family's company, CEO Eve Chevalier must accept a takeover bid from her rival, Gage Caron. And there's one term that *isn't* up for negotiation... Eve must pose as Gage's fiancée!

HPCNMRB1120

SA

Love Harlequin romance?

DISCOVER.

Be the first to find out about promotions,
news and exclusive content!

  Facebook.com/HarlequinBooks

Twitter.com/HarlequinBooks

Instagram.com/HarlequinBooks

Pinterest.com/HarlequinBooks

ReaderService.com

EXPLORE.

Sign up for the Harlequin e-newsletter and
download a free book from any series at
TryHarlequin.com

CONNECT.

Join our Harlequin community to
share your thoughts and connect
with other romance readers!
Facebook.com/groups/HarlequinConnection

HSOCIAL2020